T H̶ ̶ ̶ ̶ ̶ ̶ ̶ ̶ ̶ ̶ S

'Short stories by a master craftsman who can make you laugh and yearn to know his people – the spirited, maddening, great-hearted people of poor Ireland'
– Books and Bookmen

'brilliant and penetrating studies of young men who are either agin the government or agin religion, young women who have a struggle between their good Catholic consciences and sex, or priests who have to struggle with both'
– Oxford Mail

'Today, no Irish writer perceives the Irish as subtly: he is as needlingly accurate about provincial life as Joyce was about Dublin.'
– William Trevor in *The Guardian*

'a master'　　　　　– Stephen Wall in *The Listener*

'perfect'　　　　　– Anthony Burgess in the *Spectator*

The cover photograph shows Parliament Bridge and the Holy Trinity Church, Cork, as seen from Sullivan's Quay

By the same author in Pan Books

AN ONLY CHILD
FISH FOR FRIDAY and Other Stories
MY FATHER'S SON

FRANK O'CONNOR

THE MAD LOMASNEYS

and other stories from
Collection Two

PAN BOOKS LTD : LONDON

First published 1964 in *Collection Two* by
Macmillan and Company Ltd.
This edition (which forms Part 1) published 1970 by
Pan Books Ltd, 33 Tothill Street, London, S.W.1

ISBN 0 330 02446 9

2nd Printing 1971

© Frank O'Connor 1964

*Printed in Great Britain by
Cox & Wyman Ltd, London, Reading and Fakenham*

INTRODUCTION

This introduction was written for *Collection Two*. The second half, including 'The Little Mother' will be published in 1971 under the title *The Little Mother and other stories*.

ELEVEN YEARS ago *The Stories of Frank O'Connor* was published. By the time it was finished I had to see a specialist who took a poor view of my condition, but the book itself was a success. More important, it was a book which I could, and still can, take for granted.

This was my downfall, because I agreed to publish a successor. I worked at *More Stories* during emotional and financial troubles, and I have never been able to take it for granted. All I could do was to refuse to allow it to be published in England until I could tackle it as I felt it should be tackled. Off and on, this has taken the best part of ten years.

'Forgery' is how an eminent Irish writer has described this method of editing one's own work, but 'forgery' is not a term of literary criticism, and is, I think, an unnecessarily harsh one to describe what at worst is a harmless eccentricity. Literature is not an aspect of banking. It is true that a number of my stories have been re-written a score of times – some as many as fifty times – and re-written again and again after publication. My wife has collected copies of 'The Little Mother' she found in the wastepaper basket, but has lost count of her total, which is distributed over three countries and ten years. This is a great annoyance to some of my friends, particularly my publishers and editors, who would prefer me to write new stories instead; I am afraid it shows a certain lack of respect for one's own public image ('after all, old man, you are a professional or you aren't'); but simply as a forger I must be the greatest failure who ever lived because I forge only cheques that have already been cashed and spent.

The only criticism of this eccentricity, if I may so call it, that ever shook me was that of the editor of *The New Yorker* in which so many of these stories have appeared. He asked, 'But *can* you remember the story you set out to write?' and it is a question I still cannot answer. I believe I can remember. I believe the essence of any story can be expressed in four or five lines, but I cannot prove it. All I could possibly do would be to refer the reader to a textbook of the short story in which the earliest and latest versions of one of my stories are printed together. But this would mean taking myself a great deal too seriously, which, from my point of view, would be hardly less objectionable than not taking myself seriously enough.

For the British and Irish reader the book has split up accidentally in a way I had not planned. Exactly half of it might possibly be familiar to him, the other half should be new. It consists of stories from my first book, published thirty-two years ago, and stories I have not yet published in book form, side by side in an ideal ambiance that will be shattered by the time the book itself appears. I have lost, or never known, the confidence of the Irish poet who wrote over a thousand years ago—

> God be praised who ne'er forgets me
>   In my art so high and cold,
> And still sheds upon my verses
>   All the magic of red gold.

Dublin 1963   FRANK O'CONNOR

CONTENTS

GUESTS OF THE NATION

One

At dusk the big Englishman, Belcher, would shift his long legs out of the ashes and say 'Well, chums, what about it?' and Noble or myself would say 'All right, chum' (for we had picked up some of their curious expressions), and the little Englishman, Hawkins, would light the lamp and bring out the cards. Sometimes Jeremiah Donovan would come up and supervise the game, and get excited over Hawkins' cards, which he always played badly, and shout at him as if he was one of our own, 'Ah, you divil, why didn't you play the tray?'

But ordinarily Jeremiah was a sober and contented poor devil like the big Englishman, Belcher, and was looked up to only because he was a fair hand at documents, though he was slow even with them. He wore a small cloth hat and big gaiters over his long pants, and you seldom saw him with his hands out of his pockets. He reddened when you talked to him, tilting from toe to heel and back, and looking down all the time at his big farmer's feet. Noble and myself used to make fun of his broad accent, because we were both from the town.

I could not at the time see the point of myself and Noble guarding Belcher and Hawkins at all, for it was my belief that you could have planted that pair down anywhere from this to Claregalway and they'd have taken root there like a native weed. I never in my short experience saw two men take to the country as they did.

They were passed on to us by the Second Battalion when the search for them became too hot, and Noble and myself, being young, took them over with a natural feeling of

9

responsibility, but Hawkins made us look like fools when he showed that he knew the country better than we did.

'You're the bloke they call Bonaparte,' he says to me. 'Mary Brigid O'Connell told me to ask what you'd done with the pair of her brother's socks you borrowed.'

For it seemed, as they explained it, that the Second had little evenings, and some of the girls of the neighbourhood turned up, and, seeing they were such decent chaps, our fellows could not leave the two Englishmen out. Hawkins learned to dance *The Walls of Limerick, The Siege of Ennis* and *The Waves of Tory* as well as any of them, though he could not return the compliment, because our lads at that time did not dance foreign dances on principle.

So whatever privileges Belcher and Hawkins had with the Second they just took naturally with us, and after the first couple of days we gave up all pretence of keeping an eye on them. Not that they could have got far, because they had accents you could cut with a knife, and wore khaki tunics and overcoats with civilian pants and boots, but I believe myself they never had any idea of escaping and were quite content to be where they were.

It was a treat to see how Belcher got off with the old woman in the house where we were staying. She was a great warrant to scold, and cranky even with us, but before ever she had a chance of giving our guests, as I may call them, a lick of her tongue, Belcher had made her his friend for life. She was breaking sticks, and Belcher, who had not been more than ten minutes in the house, jumped up and went over to her.

'Allow me, madam,' he said, smiling his queer little smile. 'Please allow me,' and he took the hatchet from her. She was too surprised to speak, and after that, Belcher would be at her heels, carrying a bucket, a basket or a load of turf. As Noble said, he got into looking before she leapt, and hot water, or any little thing she wanted, Belcher would have ready for her. For such a huge man (and though I am five foot ten myself I had to look up at him) he had an uncommon lack of speech. It took us a little while to get used to him, walking in and out like a ghost, without speaking.

Especially because Hawkins talked enough for a platoon it was strange to hear Belcher with his toes in the ashes come out with a solitary 'Excuse me, chum,' or 'That's right, chum.' His one and only passion was cards, and he was a remarkably good card player. He could have skinned myself and Noble, but whatever we lost to him, Hawkins lost to us, and Hawkins only played with the money Belcher gave him.

Hawkins lost to us because he had too much old gab, and we probably lost to Belcher for the same reason. Hawkins and Noble argued about religion into the early hours of the morning, and Hawkins worried the life out of Noble, who had a brother a priest, with a string of questions that would puzzle a cardinal. Even in treating of holy subjects, Hawkins had a deplorable tongue. I never met a man who could mix such a variety of cursing and bad language into any argument. He was a terrible man, and a fright to argue. He never did a stroke of work, and when he had no one else to argue with, he got stuck in the old woman.

He met his match in her, for when he tried to get her to complain profanely of the drought she gave him a great come-down by blaming it entirely on Jupiter Pluvius (a deity neither Hawkins nor I had ever heard of, though Noble said that among the pagans it was believed that he had something to do with the rain). Another day he was swearing at the capitalists for starting the German war when the old lady laid down her iron, puckered up her little crab's mouth and said: 'Mr Hawkins, you can say what you like about the war, and think you'll deceive me because I'm only a simple poor countrywoman, but I know what started the war. It was the Italian Count that stole the heathen divinity out of the temple in Japan. Believe me, Mr Hawkins, nothing but sorrow and want can follow people who disturb the hidden powers.'

A queer old girl, all right.

Two

One evening we had our tea and Hawkins lit the lamp and we all sat into cards. Jeremiah Donovan came in too, and sat and watched us for a while, and it suddenly struck me that he had no great love for the two Englishmen. It came as a surprise to me because I had noticed nothing of it before.

Late in the evening a really terrible argument blew up between Hawkins and Noble about capitalists and priests and love of country.

'The capitalists pay the priests to tell you about the next world so that you won't notice what the bastards are up to in this,' said Hawkins.

'Nonsense, man!' said Noble, losing his temper. 'Before ever a capitalist was thought of people believed in the next world.'

Hawkins stood up as though he was preaching.

'Oh, they did, did they?' he said with a sneer. 'They believed all the things you believe – isn't that what you mean? And you believe God created Adam, and Adam created Shem, and Shem created Jehoshophat. You believe all that silly old fairytale about Eve and Eden and the apple. Well listen to me, chum! If you're entitled to a silly belief like that, I'm entitled to my own silly belief – which is that the first thing your God created was a bleeding capitalist, with morality and Rolls-Royce complete. Am I right, chum?' he says to Belcher.

'You're right, chum,' says Belcher with a smile, and he got up from the table to stretch his long legs into the fire and stroke his moustache. So, seeing that Jeremiah Donovan was going, and that there was no knowing when the argument about religion would be over, I went out with him. We strolled down to the village together, and then he stopped, blushing and mumbling, and said I should be behind, keeping guard. I didn't like the tone he took with me, and anyway I was bored with life in the cottage, so I replied by asking what the hell we wanted to guard them for at all.

He looked at me in surprise and said: 'I thought you knew we were keeping them as hostages.'

'Hostages?' I said.

'The enemy have prisoners belonging to us, and now they're talking of shooting them,' he said. 'If they shoot our prisoners, we'll shoot theirs.'

'Shoot Belcher and Hawkins?' I said.

'What else did you think we were keeping them for?' he said.

'Wasn't it very unforeseen of you not to warn Noble and myself of that in the beginning?' I said.

'How was it?' he said. 'You might have known that much.'

'We could not know it, Jeremiah Donovan,' I said. 'How could we when they were on our hands so long?'

'The enemy have our prisoners as long and longer,' he said.

'That's not the same thing at all,' said I.

'What difference is there?' said he.

I couldn't tell him, because I knew he wouldn't understand. If it was only an old dog that you had to take to the vet's, you'd try and not get too fond of him, but Jeremiah Donovan was not a man who would ever be in danger of that.

'And when is this to be decided?' I said.

'We might hear tonight,' he said. 'Or tomorrow or the next day at latest. So if it's only hanging round that's a trouble to you, you'll be free soon enough.'

It was not the hanging round that was a trouble to me at all by this time. I had worse things to worry about. When I got back to the cottage the argument was still on. Hawkins was holding forth in his best style, maintaining that there was no next world, and Noble saying that there was; but I could see that Hawkins had had the best of it.

'Do you know what, chum?' he was saying with a saucy smile. 'I think you're just as big a bleeding unbeliever as I am. You say you believe in the next world, and you know just as much about the next world as I do, which is sweet damn-all. What's heaven? You don't know. Where's heaven?

13

You don't know. You know sweet damn-all! I ask you again, do they wear wings?'

'Very well, then,' said Noble. 'They do. Is that enough for you? They do wear wings.'

'Where do they get them then? Who makes them? Have they a factory for wings? Have they a sort of store where you hand in your chit and take your bleeding wings?'

'You're an impossible man to argue with,' said Noble. 'Now, listen to me—' And they were off again.

It was long after midnight when we locked up and went to bed. As I blew out the candle I told Noble. He took it very quietly. When we'd been in bed about an hour he asked if I thought we should tell the Englishmen. I didn't, because I doubted if the English would shoot our men. Even if they did, the Brigade officers, who were always up and down to the Second Battalion and knew the Englishmen well, would hardly want to see them plugged. 'I think so too,' said Noble. 'It would be great cruelty to put the wind up them now.'

'It was very unforeseen of Jeremiah Donovan, anyhow,' said I.

It was next morning that we found it so hard to face Belcher and Hawkins. We went about the house all day, scarcely saying a word. Belcher didn't seem to notice; he was stretched into the ashes as usual, with his usual look of waiting in quietness for something unforeseen to happen, but Hawkins noticed it and put it down to Noble's being beaten in the argument of the night before.

'Why can't you take the discussion in the proper spirit?' he said severely. 'You and your Adam and Eve! I'm a Communist, that's what I am. Communist or Anarchist, it all comes to much the same thing.' And he went round the house, muttering when the fit took him: 'Adam and Eve! Adam and Eve! Nothing better to do with their time than pick bleeding apples!'

Three

I don't know how we got through that day, but I was very glad when it was over, the tea things were cleared away, and Belcher said in his peaceable way: 'Well, chums, what about it?' We sat round the table and Hawkins took out the cards, and just then I heard Jeremiah Donovan's footsteps on the path and a dark presentiment crossed my mind. I rose from the table and caught him before he reached the door.

'What do you want?' I asked.

'I want those two soldier friends of yours,' he said, getting red.

'Is that the way, Jeremiah Donovan?' I asked.

'That's the way. There were four of our lads shot this morning, one of them a boy of sixteen.'

'That's bad,' I said.

At that moment Noble followed me out, and the three of us walked down the path together, talking in whispers. Feeney, the local intelligence officer, was standing by the gate.

'What are you going to do about it?' I asked Jeremiah Donovan.

'I want you and Noble to get them out; tell them they're being shifted again; that'll be the quietest way.'

'Leave me out of that,' said Noble under his breath.

Jeremiah Donovan looked at him hard.

'All right,' he says. 'You and Feeney get a few tools from the shed and dig a hole by the far end of the bog. Bonaparte and myself will be after you. Don't let anyone see you with the tools. I wouldn't like it to go beyond ourselves.'

We saw Feeney and Noble go round to the shed and went in ourselves. I left Jeremiah Donovan to do the explanations. He told them that he had orders to send them back to the Second Battalion. Hawkins let out a mouthful of curses, and you could see that though Belcher didn't say anything, he was a bit upset too. The old woman was for having them stay in spite of us, and she didn't stop advising them until

Jeremiah Donovan lost his temper and turned on her. He had a nasty temper, I noticed. It was pitch-dark in the cottage by this time, but no one thought of lighting the lamp, and in the darkness the two Englishmen fetched their topcoats and said goodbye to the old woman.

'Just as a man makes a home of a bleeding place, some bastard at headquarters thinks you're too cushy and shunts you off,' said Hawkins, shaking her hand.

'A thousand thanks, madam,' said Belcher. 'A thousand thanks for everything' – as though he'd made it up.

We went round to the back of the house and down towards the bog. It was only then that Jeremiah Donovan told them. He was shaking with excitement.

'There were four of our fellows shot in Cork this morning and now you're to be shot as a reprisal.'

'What are you talking about?' snaps Hawkins. 'It's bad enough being mucked about as we are without having to put up with your funny jokes.'

'It isn't a joke,' says Donovan. 'I'm sorry, Hawkins, but it's true,' and begins on the usual rigmarole about duty and how unpleasant it is. I never noticed that people who talk a lot about duty find it much of a trouble to them.

'Oh, cut it out!' said Hawkins.

'Ask Bonaparte,' said Donovan, seeing that Hawkins wasn't taking him seriously. 'Isn't it true, Bonaparte?'

'It is,' I said, and Hawkins stopped.

'Ah, for Christ's sake, chum!'

'I mean it, chum,' I said.

'You don't sound as if you meant it.'

'If he doesn't mean it, I do,' said Donovan, working himself up.

'What have you against me, Jeremiah Donovan?'

'I never said I had anything against you. But why did your people take out four of your prisoners and shoot them in cold blood?'

He took Hawkins by the arm and dragged him on, but it was impossible to make him understand that we were in earnest. I had the Smith and Wesson in my pocket and I kept fingering it and wondering what I'd do if they put up a fight for it or ran, and wishing to God they'd do one or the other. I knew if they did run for it, that I'd never fire on them. Hawkins wanted to know was Noble in it, and when we said yes he asked us why Noble wanted to plug him. Why did any of us want to plug him? What had he done to us? Weren't we all chums? Didn't we understand him and didn't he understand us? Did we imagine for an instant that he'd shoot us for all the so-and-so officers in the so-and-so British Army?

By this time we'd reached the bog, and I was so sick I couldn't even answer him. We walked along the edge of it in the darkness, and every now and then Hawkins would call a halt and begin all over again, as if he was wound up, about our being chums, and I knew that nothing but the sight of the grave would convince him that we had to do it. And all the time I was hoping that something would happen; that they'd run for it or that Noble would take over the responsibility from me. I had the feeling that it was worse on Noble than on me

Four

At last we saw the lantern in the distance and made towards it. Noble was carrying it, and Feeney was standing somewhere in the darkness behind him, and the picture of them so still and silent in the bogland brought it home to me that we were in earnest, and banished the last bit of hope I had.

Belcher, on recognizing Noble, said: 'Hallo, chum,' in his quiet way, but Hawkins flew at him at once, and the argument began all over again, only this time Noble had nothing to say for himself and stood with his head down, holding the lantern between his legs.

It was Jeremiah Donovan who did the answering. For the twentieth time, as though it was haunting his mind, Hawkins asked if anybody thought he'd shoot Noble.

'Yes, you would,' said Jeremiah Donovan.

'No, I wouldn't, damn you!'

'You would, because you'd know you'd be shot for not doing it.'

'I wouldn't, not if I was to be shot twenty times over. I wouldn't shoot a pal. And Belcher wouldn't – isn't that right, Belcher?'

'That's right, chum,' Belcher said, but more by way of answering the question than of joining in the argument. Belcher sounded as though whatever unforeseen thing he'd always been waiting for had come at last.

'Anyway, who says Noble would be shot if I wasn't? What do you think I'd do if I was in his place, out in the middle of a blasted bog?'

'What would you do?' asked Donovan.

'I'd go with him wherever he was going, of course. Share my last bob with him and stick by him through thick and thin. No one can ever say of me that I let down a pal.'

'We had enough of this,' said Jeremiah Donovan, cocking his revolver. 'Is there any message you want to send?'

'No, there isn't.'

'Do you want to say your prayers?'

Hawkins came out with a cold-blooded remark that even shocked me and turned on Noble again.

'Listen to me, Noble,' he said. 'You and me are chums. You can't come over to my side, so I'll come over to your side. That show you I mean what I say? Give me a rifle and I'll go along with you and the other lads.'

Nobody answered him. We knew that was no way out.

'Hear what I'm saying?' he said. 'I'm through with it. I'm a deserter or anything else you like. I don't believe in your stuff, but it's no worse than mine. That satisfy you?'

Noble raised his head, but Donovan began to speak and he lowered it again without replying.

'For the last time, have you any messages to send?' said Donovan in a cold, excited sort of voice.

'Shut up, Donovan! You don't understand me, but these lads do. They're not the sort to make a pal and kill a pal. They're not the tools of any capitalist.'

I alone of the crowd saw Donovan raise his Webley to the back of Hawkins' neck, and as he did so I shut my eyes and tried to pray. Hawkins had begun to say something else when Donovan fired, and as I opened my eyes at the bang, I saw Hawkins stagger at the knees and lie out flat at Noble's feet, slowly and as quiet as a kid falling asleep, with the lantern-light on his lean legs and bright farmer's boots. We all stood very still, watching him settle out in the last agony.

Then Belcher took out a handkerchief and began to tie it about his own eyes (in our excitement we'd forgotten to do the same for Hawkins), and, seeing it wasn't big enough, turned and asked for the loan of mine. I gave it to him and he knotted the two together and pointed with his foot at Hawkins.

'He's not quite dead,' he said. 'Better give him another.'

Sure enough, Hawkins' left knee was beginning to rise. I bent down and put my gun to his head; then, recollecting myself, I got up again. Belcher understood what was in my mind.

'Give him his first,' he said. 'I don't mind. Poor bastard, we don't know what's happening to him now.'

I knelt and fired. By this time I didn't seem to know what I was doing. Belcher, who was fumbling a bit awkwardly with the handkerchiefs, came out with a laugh as he heard the shot. It was the first time I had heard him laugh and it sent a shudder down my back; it sounded so unnatural.

'Poor bugger!' he said quietly. 'And last night he was so curious about it all. It's very queer, chums, I always think. Now he knows as much about it as they'll ever let him know, and last night he was all in the dark.'

Donovan helped him to tie the handkerchiefs about his eyes. 'Thanks, chum,' he said. Donovan asked if there were any messages he wanted sent.

'No, chum,' he said. 'Not for me. If any of you would like to write to Hawkins' mother, you'll find a letter from her in his pocket. He and his mother were great chums. But my missus left me eight years ago. Went away with another fellow and took the kid with her. I like the feeling of a home, as you may have noticed, but I couldn't start another again after that.'

It was an extraordinary thing, but in those few minutes

Belcher said more than in all the weeks before. It was just as if the sound of the shot had started a flood of talk in him and he could go on the whole night like that, quite happily, talking about himself. We stood around like fools now that he couldn't see us any longer. Donovan looked at Noble, and Noble shook his head. Then Donovan raised his Webley, and at that moment Belcher gave his queer laugh again. He may have thought we were talking about him, or perhaps he noticed the same thing I'd noticed and couldn't understand it.

'Excuse me, chums,' he said. 'I feel I'm talking the hell of a lot, and so silly, about my being so handy about a house and things like that. But this thing came on me suddenly. You'll forgive me, I'm sure.'

'You don't want to say a prayer?' asked Donovan.

'No, chum,' he said. 'I don't think it would help. I'm ready, and you boys want to get it over.'

'You understand that we're only doing our duty?' said Donovan.

Belcher's head was raised like a blind man's, so that you could only see his chin and the top of his nose in the lantern-light.

'I never could make out what duty was myself,' he said. 'I think you're all good lads, if that's what you mean. I'm not complaining.'

Noble, just as if he couldn't bear any more of it, raised his fist at Donovan, and in a flash Donovan raised his gun and fired. The big man went over like a sack of meal, and this time there was no need of a second shot.

I don't remember much about the burying, but that it was worse than all the rest because we had to carry them to the grave. It was all mad lonely with nothing but a patch of lantern-light between ourselves and the dark, and birds hooting and screeching all round, disturbed by the guns. Noble went through Hawkins' belongings to find the letter from his mother, and then joined his hands together. He did the same with Belcher. Then, when we'd filled in the grave, we separated from Jeremiah Donovan and Feeney and took our tools back to the shed. All the way we didn't speak a word.

The kitchen was dark and cold as we'd left it, and the old woman was sitting over the hearth, saying her beads. We walked past her into the room, and Noble struck a match to light the lamp. She rose quietly and came to the doorway with all her cantankerousness gone.

'What did ye do with them?' she asked in a whisper, and Noble started so that the match went out in his hand.

'What's that?' he asked without turning round.

'I heard ye,' she said.

'What did you hear?' asked Noble.

'I heard ye. Do ye think I didn't hear ye, putting the spade back in the houseen?'

Noble struck another match and this time the lamp lit for him.

'Was that what ye did to them?' she asked.

Then, by God, in the very doorway, she fell on her knees and began praying, and after looking at her for a minute or two Noble did the same by the fireplace. I pushed my way out past her and left them at it. I stood at the door, watching the stars and listening to the shrieking of the birds dying out over the bogs. It is so strange what you feel at times like that that you can't describe it. Noble says he saw everything ten times the size, as though there were nothing in the whole world but that little patch of bog with the two Englishmen stiffening into it, but with me it was as if the patch of bog where the Englishmen were was a million miles away, and even Noble and the old woman, mumbling behind me, and the birds and the bloody stars were all far away, and I was somehow very small and very lost and lonely like a child astray in the snow. And anything that happened to me afterwards, I never felt the same about again.

Guests of the Nation (1931)

THE PROCESSION OF LIFE

One night Andy Coleman came home and found the front door locked against him. It was not the first time it had happened. Ever since his mother died six months before Andy's father had made a dead set at him. It was an extraordinary thing, just as though his mother's death had released in his father a flood of malice and jealousy that until then had been dammed up. Jealousy was the only way Andy could describe it to himself, though when he tried to think what his father had to be jealous about he couldn't put his finger on it. He had a miserable little job on the railway, few friends and no girl; but that was how things were. Watching Andy put on a tie, light a cigarette, or even brush his hair before going for his evening walk, his father seemed like a man distracted with envy. Andy knocked again, a little bit louder.

'Who's that?' his father asked from upstairs – as if he didn't know, the old bastard!

'It's me, father,' Andy replied in a low, appealing voice.

'This house is locked at ten o'clock,' his father snarled.

'Ah, for God's sake, let us in, can't you?' Andy begged.

'This house is locked at ten, I say.'

Despairingly Andy began to knock again. It was easily seen that his mother was dead. She wouldn't have lain there and left him outside, not for twenty men like his father. Now, they were both of them out. Andy was a finely-strung young fellow with a long, keen face, quick to mirth and quick to misery. Suddenly he put his hands before his eyes and began to sob, as much for his mother as himself – all her years of misery and toil, and nothing to show for it but this. A neighbour's door opened discreetly and a woman's voice whispered: 'Is anything wrong, Andy?'

'No, thanks, Mrs Walsh,' he said hastily, shaking off the boy in him. But he could not reach for a man quickly enough. He knew that now he had roused the neighbours he would only have to knock a little longer to shame his brute of a father into opening the door, but he was too sensitive to face it and the storm of abuse that would follow. He turned on his heel and went quickly down the lane. He had begun to weep again. On the road people were returning home in the early night, mellow and lingering. Only he had no home to go to.

He walked quickly in the shadow where people would be unlikely to identify him and ask the cause of his tears. One of them would have brought him home all right; he was a popular boy, well-liked because he had the friendly word for everybody, but he could not face explaining to them what a hell his life had become. His mind was full of wild schemes for running away, joining the army or taking a ship.

It was only when the storm of tears had passed over that he could consider his own plight with any reasonableness. It was obvious that he could not wander round and round the city the whole night. Some policeman would be bound to pick him up and bring him to the Bridewell, and that, in his imagination, was all bound up with courts and things in the newspapers. The only place that seemed to promise safety was the river bank. At that hour of the night it was usually deserted, and there were frequently bales of merchandise or piles of timber that a fellow could lie down between. At least, it wasn't raining.

With a sinking heart he crossed the New Bridge and faced the murk and blackness of the ill-lit quay. There were only two small boats at the jetties, and they, too, seemed deserted. He passed them, and then some storehouses and mills before he saw the gleam of a fire ahead. It was a watchman's brazier, and the watchman himself was sitting in his little sentry-box. He was a man in his late fifties or early sixties, with grey hair cropped close, a small grey moustache, a fresh, childish complexion and blue, innocent red-rimmed eyes as though the brazier smoke hurt them. He looked suspiciously at Andy.

'Goodnight, sir,' Andy said with what he always thought of as a winning smile.

The watchman looked him over again and his jaw set in an obstinate look. Andy, who was accustomed to summing up people rapidly, decided he was an obstinate old brute.

'Goodnight,' he said with finality.

'I suppose you wouldn't be able to tell me where there's any place round I could doss down for the night?' Andy asked lightly, not making too much of his trouble.

'What do you want to sleep out for, boy?' the watchman asked sternly.

'Because I'm after being locked out – that's why,' Andy replied.

'Why were you locked out?'

'I only wish I knew,' Andy said with a touch of bitterness. 'My father wouldn't give you many reasons.'

'What school do you go to?' the watchman asked, and Andy knew he was trying to find out what class of boy he was.

'Ah, I'm left school, sir,' Andy said. 'I used to go to the Monastery but I had to leave after my mother died. I'm working on the railway now.'

'This is no hour for a boy of your age to be out,' the watchman said severely.

'Oh, but I wasn't out till this hour,' Andy protested quickly. He was a boy who tended to lose his head and fly into tempers, but up to the final moment he tried to keep up a reasonable tone. 'As a matter of fact, it was hardly half past ten.'

'Half past ten is late enough,' the watchman said, refusing to yield an inch. 'Young fellows do be only getting into trouble, stopping out till all hours.'

'Well, I never got into much trouble anyhow,' Andy said with his candid, almost grown-up air. If Andy were ever to be hanged in the wrong, he would be trying to explain his innocence even with the rope round his neck. 'I mean, you know yourself the way it is. You get talking to a man at his door about one thing or another, and the time passes.'

'There is a place further down the river where you could stop,' the watchman said.

'Is that down opposite Tivoli, sir?' Andy asked.

'Yes, that is where the tramps go.'

Andy knew it well, though only from fine Sunday afternoons when his mother had taken him there; a bandstand on the river bank with trees about it; a lonesome place at that hour of night.

'You wouldn't mind me stopping here by the fire, would you, sir?' he asked gently.

'I would mind it,' the watchman replied sourly. 'I cannot have people making a rendezvous of this place. I have too much valuable property to protect.'

'You needn't worry about the property, sir,' said Andy with an affected laugh. ' 'Twould be there a long time before I'd touch it. 'Tis only while I get warm.'

'You can warm yourself, but you cannot stay,' the watchman said. 'You are a very foolish boy. It would be wiser for you to obey your father. He knows what is good for you, better than you do. But things are made too easy for young people nowadays; they expect too much. When I was your age I worked from seven in the morning till seven at night – twelve hours, and no such thing as half days either, and sixpence a week was all my father allowed me. That is the truth. Four and sixpence I had to give my mother; five shillings was all I got. Things are made too easy nowadays – pictures, cigarettes and everything.'

'To tell the truth, I never bother my head with the pictures,' Andy said, conscious at the same time that he had put a cigarette in his mouth. 'Have one of these, sir.'

'I do not smoke them,' the watchman said, shaking his head severely.

'But I don't see any harm in them, do you?' Andy asked.

'I do see harm in them. I see great harm in them. Young fellows cannot afford them at the cruel price they are sold at. A young fellow should be steady and do without things he cannot afford. I saw clever men that never learned that, and I saw what happened them. Drink, horses, women – once they start there is no end to it. I saw one professor from the college here one night, and the conduct and language of that man, there is no describing it.'

25

He began to tell of other characters he had known, a doctor on Patrick's Hill, a stockbroker, even a priest, all of whom had succumbed to temptation the way Andy was succumbing to it now, and had ended up bad. Andy listened deferentially, but all the same it struck him as queer that a man as well able to mind himself as the watchman wouldn't have done a bit better for himself in life. His conversation seemed to be one long moan, like a Good Friday service: all the same, it passed the time, and listening to Shandon strike the hours Andy was aware of the night's passing.

At last the watchman rose stiffly.

'Now you have to be going, boy,' he said. 'I have duties to attend to.'

'Ah, I'll go now, in a minute,' said Andy.

'You will go at once, boy,' the watchman said, his voice rising to a wail. 'People come round here – policemen and inspectors – and I have to mind my reputation. A man's reputation is everything.'

'Ah, for God's sake, I'm not going to do any harm to your reputation,' said Andy. He had heard the footsteps coming down the quay and hoped for better company.

'I will have no back answers from you,' the watchman said fiercely. 'Go on now where you were going, boy!'

'Oh, I'll go, I'll go,' Andy said coolly, but he had no intention of going. He moved slowly in the direction of the footsteps, and when he saw it was a woman he smiled and raised his cap.

'Is that you, Mac?' she asked in surprise.

'No, miss,' he replied with an easy laugh. 'My name is Andy Coleman. I just happened to be taking a heat at the fire.'

'Jesus!' she said. 'You gave me a start. Who are you anyway?'

'Never mind who he is or what he is,' cried the watchman. 'Leave him go back where he came from.'

'Ah, give us a breeze, Mac!' she said reproachfully. 'Can't we even pass the time of day? What are you doing here?'

'I was locked out,' Andy said with a shrug, but he noticed

himself the way his tone had changed. It was more light-hearted, as if being locked out were an everyday occurrence with him.

'Sit down and tell us about it,' she said. 'Mac, are we going to get that cup of tea?'

'Ah, I have something better to do than be making tea for night-walkers like that,' the watchman said with an indignant quaver in his voice.

The woman collapsed on to a box by the brazier.

'God, am I not to be allowed to talk to the boy for two minutes?' she cried. 'Or what sort of old fool are you at all? Will you put that billy can on for the love of God, and give us less of your old gab.'

She was a big, blowsy woman with the remains of her good looks still about her, and something pleasant and musical in her loud, hoarse, scolding voice. The watchman looked at her, trembling with rage, his blue eyes with their raw surrounds looking as though at any moment he might burst into tears. Then he shook his head at no one in particular and put the billy can on to boil.

'Sit down and tell us about yourself,' she said, making room for Andy.

'Ah, there isn't much to tell,' Andy said. 'I came home at half ten, and my old fellow had the house locked up and wouldn't let me in.'

'And wasn't there anyone to open the door for you?'

'Ah, no. I'm an only child.'

'And what about your mother?'

'She died a few months ago. I had to leave school, and 'tis since then all the trouble started.'

'I suppose he can do what he likes now,' she said bitterly.

'He might have his reasons,' the watchman said, addressing nobody in particular.

'Ah, 'tis easy the talk comes to you,' she said shrilly. ' 'Tis a hard day for a child when he leaves his mother in the graveyard and comes back to live with his father. Bloody misfortunate brutes! I seen too much of them.'

'You know nothing about it,' the watchman said violently.

'Don't I? I suppose I don't know what happened the

houseful of us after we left my poor mother up in the Botanics? It wasn't long before she had company either.'

'I say it's not fair to judge a man you do not know,' said the watchman. 'Men have great responsibilities that women know nothing about.'

'They have, I hear!' she retorted mockingly. 'Like my old fellow. The only responsibility he ever had was to see that his kids wouldn't have enough to eat for fear the publicans would go short, and he done that like a right true Christian. Bloody old brute! God forgive me!'

'It is not right to talk like that,' the watchman said as he poured a paper of tea into the can.

'What's wrong about it?'

'Encouraging young fellows to talk like that about their fathers. Little enough respect they have.'

'And what respect could they have and the way they're treated? If that child got his death of cold, I'll guarantee his father wouldn't care much.'

'Even so, even so,' the watchman said sourly. 'My own father was a severe man, but I never talked against him like that.'

'Your own sons weren't so obliging, though.'

'That is what I mean,' he said with sudden dignity.

'And what the hell do you expect? Wanting to marry again at your age with an old floosie like Mollie Anderson?'

'Whatever I might do, I am entitled to respect,' the watchman said in a bigoted tone. 'You do not raise your hand to your father without paying for it sooner or later.'

'Send us word when pay day comes round,' she said with sudden pity. 'Don't you believe it, Mac. They'll be warming their ass in corporation jobs when you're dying in the workhouse . . . Ah, Christ, sure I'm only talking,' she added with sudden despair. ' 'Tis a hard bloody old life, whatever way you look at it. When you're young you're walked on, and when you're old you're in the way. You might as well enjoy it while you can . . . What are you going to do?' she asked Andy in a whisper, almost without moving her lips. 'Never mind Mac. He's as deaf as a post.'

'To tell you the God's truth I don't know,' Andy replied

in the same way. 'If I could stop here for another hour or so, I'd be all right.'

'Would you like to come home with me?'

'That'd be grand,' he said with a shy smile.

'God knows, 'tisn't much, but 'tis better than this,' she said sadly. The watchman filled three jam jars with tea and passed them round.

'Was Guard Dunphy round at all, Mac?' she asked.

'No,' the watchman said sourly, 'I didn't see him these ten days.'

'With the help of God he might be shifted,' she said piously. 'He'd be a small loss . . . This is a policeman,' she said to Andy. 'He goes on his holidays to the Cistercians. He'd have you demented with Father Prissy and Father Prossy. Biggest old ram in Cork, and he's never out of churches and chapels. He'd cure you of religion.'

They drank their tea while the woman chattered on. The city bells sounded clearer as the darkness began to thin away beyond the cliffs at the farther side of the river. At last the woman rose.

'Come on, child,' she said, giving Andy her hand. 'I may as well get you back to the old doss or you'll be on my hands tomorrow.'

'What's that?' the watchman asked incredulously, raising his head.

'The boy,' she said shortly. 'I'm taking him back to let him have a few hours' sleep before he goes to work.'

'To corrupt him, you mean?' the watchman said, raising his voice.

'What the hell do you mean, corrupt him?' she shouted. 'At least, I'm not trying to throw him into the gutter the way you are. You and your dirty old mind!'

He rose, staring at her, and his head began to shake again.

'Very well!' he said in a low voice, pointing dramatically up the quay. 'Go! But don't ever come back here again! Don't turn to me for anything again, the longest day you live!'

'Ah, what ails you, you old fool?' she asked.

'Not the longest day you live,' he said in a heart-broken voice. 'It is my own fault. I knew what you were the first day I met you. I put myself out to oblige you, and this is my thanks.'

'Ah, Mac,' she said in a wail, 'don't be going on like that, for the love of God. You'll only upset yourself.'

'Go away, woman, go away!' he said.

Andy saw with interest that there were real tears in the old man's eyes. A new feeling of confidence and excitement welled up in him. He took the woman's arm and squeezed it to his side.

'Come on if you're coming,' he said. He was astonished by her whispered reply.

'Ah, for God's sake!' she said impatiently. 'Can't you see the poor divil is lonely?'

At the same moment they heard heavy footsteps, approaching from the river walk.

'Christ, come on!' she said, but she was too late. The light of the brazier caught the buttons on a policeman's uniform as he moved towards them at a comfortable stride, his cap slightly to one side of his head.

'The bloody bastard I'm trying to dodge the whole time!' she whispered despairingly, and then in a terrible voice: 'Bad luck and end to you, you sanctimonious ould ram!'

'God bless all here,' the policeman said piously.

'Ah, and you too, Guard Dunphy,' she replied.

'What's going on here?' the policeman asked, looking first at the watchman and then at Andy.

'Ah, nothing, guard,' she replied. 'Only a young fellow I was trying to get an old doss for.'

'What hurry is there?' the policeman asked as he took a packet of cigarettes from the pocket of his tunic. 'Isn't the night long? Who is it?'

'Just a friend of mine, guard.'

'If he's a friend of yours he's all right,' the policeman said. 'What did you say his name was?'

'Coleman, guard,' Andy chipped in uneasily. 'Andy Coleman.'

'And tell me, Andy, what has you out to this hour of night?'

'He was locked out,' the woman said shortly.

'Locked out?' the policeman said in surprise. 'Who locked him out?'

'Who the hell do you think only his father?' she asked. 'The poor unfortunate boy have to be at work in the morning, and I was going to get him a bed somewhere.'

'Time enough! Time enough! Take a fag and sit down for a minute.' As she did so, he turned on Andy again. 'What did he lock you out for?'

'Nothing, guard,' said Andy, his new confidence beginning to ebb. He wasn't really afraid of the guard; he didn't think the guard was a bad man, but he had a strong notion that the guard had a warm welcome for himself.

'Was it drink, tell me?'

'No, guard,' Andy said with a watchful smile. 'I never drink.'

'Horses?'

'No. I don't bet.'

'Then it could only be one other thing,' said the policeman. 'And that is something I would most strongly advise you against.'

'You'd be the one that would be well able to advise him,' the woman said curtly.

'I would. It is a thing I would advise any young fellow against. Do you know what I was doing for the last week, Lena?'

'Ah, I do not.'

'You wouldn't believe me. I was at a retreat.'

'Was this the Cistercians again?'

'It was not the Cistercians. The Cistercians do not give retreats here. What sort of old heretic are you? This was the Redemptorists. They're the boys to put the fear of God into you. I wouldn't say anything against the other orders, but when it comes to hellfire, they're only like "I roved out".'

'Well, I hope the hellfire did you good.'

'It did me great good. There is nothing in the world I like better than a good sermon. Except a hurling match . . .

Not comparing them, of course ... I didn't see you at the match on Sunday, Mac.'

'No, guard,' said the watchman. 'I was not there. What sort of match was it?'

'Rotten.'

'So I heard.'

'The rottenest match I saw in years. That team of the Barrs was not fit to send against a girls' school ... Well, Lena, what about that little walk we were going to take?'

'And what would the holy fathers say about that?' the woman asked with ill-concealed acerbity. It was lost on the policeman though.

'Ah, the holy fathers are men like ourselves,' he replied complacently. ' "Sins against Faith are serious, sins against morals, sure we all commit them." Some great Corkman said that, if only I could remember his name. Don't you agree with me, Mac?'

'I knew that fellow's father well,' said the watchman.

'Look, guard, I'll be back to you,' the woman said desperately. 'I only want to get the kid settled for the night. I won't be more than ten minutes.'

'Ah, Andy here is all right,' said the policeman in the same jovial authoritative tone, which, for some reason, reminded Andy of a priest's. 'Andy and Mac will be company for one another ... I wouldn't be down here too often, young fellow,' he added gaily to Andy. 'There's bad company round here. Goodnight, Mac.'

'Goodnight, Guard Dunphy,' the watchman said.

With a wry face, the woman took his arm, and soon the pair of them were lost in the darkness. Andy sat on for a few minutes, but the watchman did not speak.

'I think I might as well be going home,' Andy said at last.

'You might as well stop as you're here,' the watchman said despondently. 'One of them might be back.'

'I doubt it,' said Andy. 'I might as well be making for home. Goodnight and – thanks.'

The watchman did not reply, and Andy set off slowly in the direction of the city. The dawn was breaking over the cliffs to his right across the river, and buildings and ships began to emerge from the shadows. Soon a single spot of light reached out and struck the sleeping city, and in a curious way Andy's heart felt lighter. He knew he wasn't as good a boy as he had been when he came down but he felt better prepared to deal with his father and the rest that life might have in store for him. His life had been too sheltered, too much under the wing of a woman who was now under the ground. Now, the world stretched ahead of him, different from what he had imagined it, different from what it seemed by daylight, lit up with the spectral intensity of the night.

Guests of the Nation (1931)

'THE STAR THAT BIDS THE SHEPHERD FOLD'

Father Whelan, the parish priest, called on his curate, Father Devine, one evening in autumn. Father Whelan was a tall, stout man with a broad chest, a head that did not detach itself too clearly from the rest of his body, bushes of wild hair in his ears, and the rosy, innocent, good-natured face of a pious old countrywoman who made a living by selling eggs.

Devine was pale and worn-looking, with a gentle, dreamy face that had the soft gleam of an old piano keyboard, and he wore pince-nez perched on his unhappy, insignificant nose. He and Whelan got on all right considering – well, considering that Devine, who didn't know when he was well-off, had fathered a dramatic society and an annual festival on Whelan, and that, whenever his curate's name was mentioned, the parish priest – a charitable old man who never said an unkind word about anybody – tapped his head and said poor Devine's poor father was just the same. 'A national teacher – sure, I knew him well, poor man!'

What Devine said about Whelan in that crucified drawl of his mainly consisted of the old man's own words, with just the faintest inflection to underline their fatuity. 'I know some of the clergy are very opposed to books, but I like a book myself. I am very fond of Zane Grey. Zane Grey is an author I would recommend to anybody, father. Even poetry I like. Some of the poems you see on advertisements are very clever.' Devine was clever; he was lonely; he had a few good original water-colours and a bookcase full of works that were a constant source of wonder to the parish priest. Whelan stood in front of them now, his hat in his hands, his glasses raised, lifting his warty old nose while his eyes were as blank and hopeless as his charity.

'Nothing there in your line, I'm afraid,' Devine said with his maddeningly respectful, deprecating air, as if he really put the parish priest's taste on a level with his own.

' 'Tisn't that at all,' Whelan said in a mournful, faraway voice. 'Only you have a lot of foreign books. I suppose you know the languages well.'

'Well enough to read,' Devine said wearily, his handsome head on one side. 'Why?'

'That foreign boat at the jetties,' Whelan said without looking round. 'What is it? French or German or something. There's terrible scandal about it.'

'Is that so?' drawled Devine. 'I didn't hear.'

'Oh, terrible,' Whelan said mournfully, turning on him the full battery of his round, rosy old face and shining spectacles. 'There's girls on it every night. I told Sullivan I'd go round and hunt them out. It occurred to me we might want someone to speak the language.'

'I'm afraid my French would hardly rise to that,' Devine said dryly, but he made no further objection, for, except for his old-womanly fits of virtue, Whelan was all right as parish priests go. Devine had had sad experience of how they could go. He put on his faded old coat and clamped his battered hat down over his pince-nez, and the two priests went down Main Street to the post office corner. It was deserted, but for two out-of-works supporting either side of the door like ornaments, and a few others hanging hypnotized over the bridge while they studied the foaming waters of the weir. Devine had taken up carpentry in an attempt to lure them into the technical school classes, but it hadn't worked too well.

'The dear knows, you'd hardly wonder where those girls would go,' he said thoughtfully.

'Ah, what do they want to go anywhere for?' asked the parish priest, holding his head as though it were a flower-pot that might fall and break. 'They're mad on pleasure. That girl, Nora Fitzpatrick, is one of them, and her mother dying at home.'

'That might be her reason,' said Devine, who, unlike the parish priest, called at the Fitzpatricks and knew what their home was like, with six children and a mother dying of cancer.

'Ah, her place is at home, father,' Whelan said without rancour.

They went past the Technical School to the quays, deserted but for a coal boat and the big foreign grain boat which rose high and dark above the edge of the jetty on a full tide. The town was historically reputed to have been a great place, and had masses of grey stone warehouses, all staring with sightless eyes across the river. Two men who had been standing against the wall, looking up at the grain boat, came to join them. One was a tall, gaunt man with a long, sour, melancholy face which looked particularly hideous because he had a youthful pink and white complexion, and it made him resemble an old hag, heavily made up. He wore a wig and carried a rolled-up umbrella behind his back. His name was Sullivan; he was manager of a shop in town and a man Devine loathed. The other man, Joe Sheridan, was small, fat, and Jewish-looking with dark skin and an excitable manner. He was the inevitable local windbag, who lived in a perpetual hang-over from his own bouts of self-importance. As the four men met, Devine looked up and saw two young foreign faces, propped on their hands, peering over the edge of the boat.

'Well, boys?' Whelan asked boldly.

'There's two of them on board at present, father,' Sullivan

said in a shrill, scolding voice. 'Nora Fitzpatrick and Phillie O'Malley. They're the worst of the lot.'

'Well, I think you'd better go on board and tell them to come out here to me,' said Whelan.

'I was wondering what our legal position was, father?' Sheridan said with mock thoughtfulness. 'I mean, have we any sort of *locus standi*?'

'Oh, if they stabbed you, or cut your throat, I think they could be tried for it,' Devine replied with bland malice. 'Of course, I don't know if your family would be entitled to compensation.'

The malice was lost on Whelan, who laid one hairy paw on Devine's shoulder, and the other on Sheridan's to soothe their fears. He exuded pious confidence. It was the eggs all over again. God would look after His hens!

'Never mind about the legal position,' he said paternally. 'I'll be answerable for that.'

'That's enough for me, father,' said Sheridan, straightening himself proudly, and then he pulled his hat down over his eyes and joined his hands behind his back before striding up the gangway, with the air of a detective in a bad American film. Sullivan, clutching his umbrella comfortingly against his back bone, strutted after him, head in air. A lovely pair, Devine thought. They went up to the two sailors.

'Two girls,' Sullivan said in his shrill voice. 'We're looking for the two girls who came on board half an hour ago.'

Neither of the sailors stirred. One turned his eyes lazily and looked Sullivan up and down.

'Not this boat,' he said insolently. 'The other. There are always girls on that.'

Then Sheridan, who had glanced down a companionway, gave tongue.

'Phillie O'Malley!' he shouted. 'Come out here to Father Whelan! He wants to talk to you.'

Nothing happened for a minute or two. Then a tall girl with a consumptive face emerged on deck with a handkerchief pressed to her eyes. Devine couldn't help feeling sick at the sight of her wretched finery, her cheap hat and bead

36

necklace. He was angry and ashamed, and a cold fury of sarcasm rose in him. The Good Shepherd, indeed!

'Come on, lads!' shouted Whelan encouragingly. 'What about the other one?'

Sheridan, flushed with triumph, was about to disappear down the companionway when one of the sailors gave him a heave that threw him to the edge of the ship. Then the sailor stood nonchalantly in the doorway, blocking the way. Whelan grew red with anger, and he only waited for the girl to leave the gangway before he went up himself. Devine paused to whisper to her.

'Get off home as quick as you can, Phillie,' he said. 'And don't be upsetting yourself about it.'

At the real tenderness in his voice she took the handkerchief from her face and began to weep in earnest, tossing her silly little head from side to side. Devine went slowly after the others. It was a ridiculous scene; the fat old priest, his head in the air, trembling with senile astonishment and anger at being blocked.

'Get out of my way, you lout!' he said.

'Don't be a fool, man!' Devine whispered with quiet ferocity. 'They're not accustomed to being spoken to like that. If you got a knife in your ribs, it would be your own fault. We want to talk to the captain.' And then, bending forward with his eyebrows raised, he asked politely: 'Would you be good enough to tell the captain we'd like to see him.'

The sailor who was blocking the way looked at him for a moment and then nodded in the direction of the upper deck. Taking Whelan's arm and telling the others to stay behind, Devine went up the ship. The second sailor passed them out, knocked at a door and said something Devine couldn't catch. Then with a scowl he held the door open.

The captain was a middle-aged man with a heavily-lined, sallow face, close-cropped hair and a black moustache. There was something Mediterranean about his air.

'Bonsoir, messieurs,' he said in a loud, businesslike tone that did not conceal a certain anxiety.

'Bonsoir, monsieur le capitaine,' Devine said with the same plaintive, ingratiating air as he bowed and raised his battered old hat. *'Est-ce que nous vous dérangeons?'*

'Mais, pas du tout; entrez, je vous prie,' the captain said heartily, clearly relieved by Devine's amiability. *'Vous parlez français, alors?'*

'Un peu, monsieur le capitaine,' Devine said modestly. *'Vous savez, ici en Irlande on n'a pas souvent l'occasion.'*

'Ah, well, I speak English good enough,' the captain said cheerfully. 'Won't you sit down?'

'I wish my French were anything as good as your English,' Devine said as he sat down.

'One travels a good deal,' said the captain with a shrug, but he was pleased just the same. 'You'll have a drink. Some brandy, eh?'

'I'd be delighted, of course, but we have a favour to ask you first.'

'A favour?' the captain said enthusiastically. 'Certainly, certainly. Anything I can do. Have a cigar?'

'Never smoke them,' Whelan said sullenly, and to mask his rudeness, Devine, who never smoked cigars, took one and lit it.

'I'd better explain who we are,' he said, sitting back, his head on one side, his long delicate hands hanging over the arms of the chair. 'This is Father Whelan, the parish priest. My name is Devine: I'm the curate.'

'And mine is Platon Demarrais,' the captain said proudly. 'I bet you never before heard of someone called Platon?'

'A relation of the philosopher, I presume,' said Devine.

'And I have two brothers, Zenon and Plotin!'

'Quite an intellectual family.'

'Pagans, of course,' the captain explained complacently. 'Greeks. My father was a schoolteacher. He called us that to annoy the priest. He was anti-clerical.'

'That isn't confined to schoolteachers in France,' Devine said dryly. 'My father was a schoolteacher too, but he never got round to calling me Aristotle. Which might be as well,' he added with a chuckle. 'At any rate, there's a girl called Fitzpatrick on the ship, with some sailor, I suppose. She's one of Father Whelan's parishioners, and we'd be grateful if you'd have her put off.'

'Speak for yourself, father,' said Whelan, raising his stubborn old peasant head and quelling fraternization with a glance. 'I wouldn't be grateful to anyone for doing what 'tis his simple duty to do.'

'Then perhaps you'd better explain your errand yourself, Father Whelan,' Devine said with an abnegation that wasn't far removed from positive waspishness.

'I think so, father,' said Whelan, unaware of the rebuke. 'That girl, Captain Whatever-your-name-is, has no business to be on your ship at all. It is no place for a young unmarried girl to be at this hour of night.'

'I don't understand,' the captain said uneasily, with a sideway glance at Devine that begged for an interpreter. 'This girl is a relative of yours?'

'No, sir,' Whelan said emphatically. 'She's nothing whatever to me.'

'Then I don't see what you want with her,' said the captain.

'That's only as I'd expect, sir,' Whelan replied boorishly.

'Oh, for Heaven's sake!' Devine interrupted impatiently. 'We'll be here all night at this rate ... You see, captain,' he said patiently, bending forward with his anxious air, his head tilted back so that the pince-nez wouldn't fall off, 'this girl is one of Father Whelan's parishioners. She's not a very good girl – I don't mean there's any harm in her,' he added hastily, catching the censoriousness in the words and feeling ashamed of himself. 'It's just that she's a bit wild. It's Father Whelan's duty to keep her out of temptation so far as he can. He is a shepherd, and she is one of his sheep,' he added with a faint smile at his own eloquence.

The captain bent forward and touched him lightly on the knee.

'You're a funny race,' he said with interest. 'All over the world I meet Englishmen, and you are all the same, and I will never understand you. Never!'

'We're not Englishmen,' Whelan said with the first trace of animation he had shown. 'Don't you know what country you're in? This is Ireland.'

'Same thing,' said the captain.

'It is not the same thing,' said Whelan.

'Pooh!' snorted the captain.

'Surely, captain,' Devine protested gently, 'we admit some distinction.'

'Distinction?' the captain said. 'What distinction?'

'At the Battle of the Boyne you fought for us,' Devine said persuasively. 'We fought for you at Fontenoy and Ramillies.

> *When on Ramillies' bloody field*
> *The baffled French were forced to yield,*
> *The victor Saxons backward reeled*
> *Before the shock of Clare's Dragoons.'*

He recited the lines with the same apologetic smile he had worn when speaking of sheep and shepherds, but they seemed to have no effect on the captain.

'No, no, no,' he cried. 'There is no difference. No difference at all. You call yourselves Irish, the others call themselves Scotch, but you are all English. It is always the same: always women, always hypocrisy, always excuses. *Toujours des excuses!* Who is this girl? The *curé*'s daughter?'

'The *curé*'s daughter?' Devine repeated in surprise.

'Whose daughter?' Whelan asked with his mouth hanging open.

'Yours, I gather,' Devine said dryly.

'Well, well, well!' the old man said, blushing. 'What sort of upbringing do they have? Does he even know we can't get married?'

'That, I should say, he takes for granted,' replied Devine over his shoulder. '*Elle n'est pas sa fille,*' he added with amusement to the captain.

'*C'est sûr?*'

'*C'est certain.*'

'*Sa maitresse alors?*'

'*Ni cela non plus,*' Devine replied evenly with only the faintest of smiles on the worn shell of his face.

'*Ah, bon, bon, bon!*' the captain said excitedly, springing from his seat and striding about the cabin, scowling and waving his arms. '*Vous vous moquez de moi, monsieur le curé. Comprenez donc, c'est seulement par politesse que j'ai voulu faire croire que c'était sa fille. On voit bien que le vieux est jaloux. Est-ce que je n'ai pas vu les flics qui surveillent mon bateau toute la semaine? Mais croyez-moi, monsieur, je me fiche de lui et de ses agents.'*

'He seems very excited about something,' Whelan said with distaste. 'What's he saying?'

'I'm trying to persuade him that she's not your mistress now,' Devine could not refrain from saying with quiet malice.

'My what?'

'Your mistress. The woman he thinks you live with. He says you're jealous and that you've had detectives watching his ship for a week.'

The blush which had risen to the old man's face now began to spread to his neck and ears, and when he spoke, his voice quavered with real emotion.

'We'd better go home, father,' he said. ' 'Tis useless talking to that man. He's either mad or bad.'

'He seems to think exactly the same of us,' said Devine as he rose. *'Venez manger demain soir et je vous expliquerai tout,'* he added to the captain.

'Je vous remercie, monsieur,' the captain replied with a shrug. *'Mais je n'ai pas besoin d'explications. Il n'y a rien d'inattendu, mais vous en faites toute une histoire.'* He clapped his hand jovially on Devine's shoulder and almost embraced him. *'Naturellement – je vous rends la fille, parce que vous la demandez, mais comprenez bien que je fais à cause de vous, et non pas à cause de monsieur et de ses agents.'* He drew himself up to his full height and glared at the parish priest, who stood in a dumb stupor like a cow just fallen from a cliff.

'Oh, quant à moi, vous feriez mieux en l'emmenant où vous allez,' Devine said with weary humour. *'Moi-même, aussi, parbleu!'*

'Quoi? Vous l'aimez aussi?' shouted the captain in desperation.

'No, no, no, no,' Devine said good-humouredly, patting him on the arm. 'It's all too complicated. I wouldn't try to understand it if I were you.'

'What's he saying now?' Whelan asked with some suspicion.

'Oh, it seems he thinks she's my mistress as well,' Devine replied pleasantly. 'He thinks we're sharing her.'

'Come on, come on!' Whelan said despairingly. 'My goodness, even I never thought they were as bad as that. And we sending missions to the blacks!'

Meanwhile, the captain had rushed aft and shouted down the companionway. A second girl appeared, also weeping, and the captain, quite moved, slapped her encouragingly on the shoulder and said something in a gruff voice which Devine didn't hear. Either he was telling her to choose younger lovers for the future or advising her to come back when the coast was clear. Devine hoped it was the latter. Then the captain went up bristling to Sullivan, who stood by the gangway, leaning on his rolled-up umbrella, and ordered him rudely off the vessel.

'*Allez-vous-en!*' he said curtly. '*Allez, allez, allez!*'

Sullivan and Sheridan went first. Dusk had crept suddenly along the quay and lay heaped there coloured like blown sand. Over the bright river mouth, shining under a bank of cloud, one lonely star twinkled. 'The star that bids the shepherd fold,' Devine thought with mournful humour. He felt hopeless and lost. Whelan preceded him down the gangway with his old woman's dull face sunk in his broad barrel chest. At the foot he stopped and looked back at the captain, who was scowling fiercely over the ship's side.

'Anyway, thanks be to the almighty God that your accursed race is withering off the face of the earth,' he said heavily.

Devine, with a rueful smile, raised his battered old hat and pulled the skirts of his coat about him as he stepped down the gangway.

'*Vous viendrez demain, monsieur le capitaine?*' he asked gently.

'*Avec plaisir. A demain, Monsieur le berger,*' replied the captain with a knowing look.

Crab Apple Jelly (1944)

THE MAD LOMASNEYS

One

Ned Lowry and Rita Lomasney had, one might say, been
lovers from childhood. The first time they had met was
when he was fourteen and she a year or two younger. It was
on the North Mall on a Saturday afternoon, and she was sitting on a bench by the river under the trees; a tall, bony
string of a girl with a long-obstinate jaw. Ned was a stu-
dious-looking young fellow in a blue and white college cap –
thin, pale and spectacled. As he passed he looked at her
owlishly, and she gave him back an impudent stare. This
upset him – he had no experience of girls – so he blushed
and raised his cap. At this she seemed to relent.

'Hullo,' she said experimentally.

'Good afternoon,' he replied with a pale, prissy smile.

'Where are you off to?' she asked.

'Oh, just up the Dyke for a walk.'

'Sit down,' she said in a sharp voice, laying her hand on
the bench beside her, and he did as he was told. It was a
summer evening, and the white quay walls and tall, crazy,
claret-coloured tenements under a blue and white sky were
reflected in the lazy water, which wrinkled only at the edges
and seemed like a painted carpet.

'It's very pleasant here,' he said complacently.

'Is it?' she asked with a truculence that startled him. 'I
don't see anything very pleasant about it.'

'Oh, it's very nice and quiet,' he said in mild surprise as he
raised his fair eyebrows and looked up and down the Mall.
'My name is Lowry,' he added politely.

'Are ye the ones that have the jewellers' shop on the Parade?' she asked.

'That's right,' he replied with modest pride.

'We have a clock we got from ye,' she said. ' 'Tisn't much
good of an old clock either,' she added with quiet malice.

'You should bring it back to the shop,' he said with concern. 'It probably needs overhauling.'

'I'm going down the river in a boat with a couple of fellows,' she said, going off at a tangent. 'Will you come?'

'Couldn't,' he said with a smile.

'Why not?'

'I'm only left go up the Dyke for a walk,' he replied complacently. 'On Saturdays I go to Confession at St Peter and Paul's; then I go up the Dyke and come back the Western Road. Sometimes you see very good cricket matches. Do you like cricket?'

'A lot of old sissies pucking a ball!' she said shortly. 'I do not.'

'I like it,' he said firmly. 'I go up there every Saturday when it's fine. Of course, I'm not supposed to talk to anyone,' he added with mild amusement at his own audacity.

'Why not?'

'My mother doesn't like me to.'

'Why doesn't she?'

'She comes of an awfully good family,' he answered mildly, and but for his gentle smile she might have thought he was deliberately insulting her. 'You see,' he went on gravely in his thin, pleasant voice, ticking things off on his fingers and then glancing at each finger individually as he ticked it off – a tidy sort of boy – 'there are three main branches of the Hourigan family: the Neddy Neds, the Neddy Jerrys, and the Neddy Thomases. The Neddy Neds are the Hayfield Hourigans. They are the oldest branch. My mother is a Hayfield Hourigan, and she'd have been a rich woman only for her father backing a bill for a Neddy Jerry. He defaulted and ran away to Australia,' he concluded with a contemptuous sniff.

'Cripes!' said the girl. 'And had she to pay?'

'She had. But of course,' he went on with as close as he ever seemed likely to get to a burst of real enthusiasm, 'my grandfather was a very well-behaved man. When he was eating his dinner the boys from the National School in Bantry used to be brought up to watch him, he had such beautiful table manners. Once he caught my uncle eating cabbage with a knife, and he struck him with a poker. They had to put four stitches in him after,' he added with a joyous chuckle.

'Cripes! 'said the girl again. 'What did he do that for?'

'To teach him manners,' Ned said earnestly.

'That's a queer way to teach him manners. He must have been dotty.'

'Oh, I wouldn't say that,' Ned said, a bit ruffled. Everything this girl said seemed to come as a shock to him. 'But that's why my mother won't let us mix with other children. On the other hand, we read a good deal. Are you fond of reading, Miss – I didn't catch the name.'

'You weren't told it,' she said quietly, showing her claws. 'But, if you want to know, it's Rita Lomasney.'

'Do you read much, Miss Lomasney?'

'I couldn't be bothered.'

'I read everything,' he said enthusiastically. 'And as well as that, I'm learning the violin from Miss Maude on the Parade. Of course, it's very difficult, because it's all classical music.'

'What's that?'

'*Maritana* is classical music,' he said eagerly. He was a bit of a puzzle to Rita. She had never before met anyone who had such a passion for teaching. 'Were you at *Maritana* in the Opera House, Miss Lomasney?'

'I was never there at all,' she said curtly, humiliated.

'And *Alice Where Art Thou* is classical music,' he added. 'It's harder than plain music. It has signs like this on it' – he began to draw things on the air – 'and when you see the signs, you know it's after turning into a different tune, though it has the same name. Irish music is all the same tune and that's why my mother won't let us learn it.'

'Were you ever at the Opera in Paris?' she asked suddenly.

'No,' said Ned with regret. 'I was never in Paris. Were you?'

'That's where you ought to go,' she said with airy enthusiasm. 'You couldn't hear any operas here. The staircase alone is bigger than the whole Opera House here.'

It seemed as if they were in for a really informative conversation when two fellows came down Wyse's Hill. Rita got up to meet them. Ned looked up at them for a moment and then rose too, lifting his college cap politely.

'Well, good afternoon,' he said cheerfully. 'I enjoyed the talk. I hope we meet again.'

'Some other Saturday,' said Rita with regret. By this time she would readily have gone up the Dyke and even watched cricket with him if he asked her.

'Oh, good evening, old man,' one of the fellows said in an affected English accent, pretending to raise a top hat. 'Do come and see us soon again.'

'Shut up, Foster, or I'll give you a puck in the gob!' Rita said sharply.

'Oh, by the way,' Ned said, returning to hand her a number of the *Gem*, which he took from his jacket pocket, 'you might like to look at this. It's not bad.'

'I'd love to,' she said insincerely, and he smiled and touched his cap again. Then with a polite and almost deferential air he went up to Foster. 'Did you say something?' he asked.

Foster looked as astonished as though a kitten had suddenly got up on his hind legs and challenged him to fight.

'I did not,' he said, and backed away.

'I'm glad,' Ned said, almost purring. 'I was afraid you might be looking for trouble.'

It astonished Rita. 'There's a queer one for you!' she said when Ned had gone. But she was curiously pleased to see that he was no sissy. She didn't like sissies.

Two

The Lomasneys lived on Sunday's Well in a small house with a long sloping garden and a fine view of the river and the city. Harry Lomasney, the builder, was a small man who wore grey tweed suits and soft collars several sizes too big for him. He had a ravaged brick-red face with keen blue eyes, and a sandy straggling moustache with one side going up and the other down, and the workmen said you could tell what humour he was in by the side he pulled. He was nicknamed 'Hasty Harry'. 'Great God!' he fumed when his wife was having her first baby. 'Nine months over a little job like that! I'd do it in three weeks if I could get started.'

His wife was tall and matronly and very pious, but her piety never got much in her way. A woman who had survived Hasty would have survived anything. Their eldest daughter, Kitty, was loud-voiced and gay, and had been expelled from school for writing indecent letters to a boy. She had failed to tell the nuns that she had copied the letters out of a French novel and didn't know what they meant. Nellie was placider than her sister and took more after her mother; besides, she didn't read French novels.

Rita was the exception among the girls. She seemed to have no softness, never had a favourite saint or a favourite nun, and said it was soppy. For the same reason she never had flirtations. Her friendship with Ned Lowry was the nearest she got to that, and though Ned came regularly to the house and took her to the pictures every week, her sisters would have found it hard to say if she ever did anything with him she wouldn't do with a girl. There was something tongue-tied, twisted, and unhappy in her. She had a curious, raw, almost timid smile as though she thought people only intended to hurt her. At home she was reserved, watchful, mocking. She could listen for hours to her mother and sisters without opening her mouth, and then suddenly mystify them by dropping a well-aimed jaw-breaker – about classical music, for instance – before relapsing into sulky silence, as though she had merely drawn back the veil for a moment on depths in herself she would not permit them to explore. This annoyed her sisters, because they knew there weren't any depths; it was all swank.

After taking her degree, she got a job in a convent school in a provincial town in the west of Ireland. She and Ned corresponded, and he even went to see her there. At home he reported that she seemed quite happy.

But it didn't last. A few months later, the Lomasneys were at supper when they heard a car stop; the gate squeaked, and steps came up the long path to the front door. Then came the bell and a cheerful voice from the hall.

'Hullo, Paschal, I suppose ye weren't expecting me?'

' 'Tis never Rita!' said her mother, meaning that it was but shouldn't be.

'As true as God, that one is after getting into trouble,' said Kitty prophetically.

The door opened and Rita slouched in; a long, stringy girl with a dark, glowing face. She kissed her father and mother lightly.

'What happened you at all, child?' her mother asked placidly.

'Nothing,' replied Rita, an octave up the scale. 'I just got the sack.'

'The sack?' said her father, beginning to pull the wrong side of his moustache. 'What did you get the sack for?' Hasty would sack a man three times in a day, but nobody paid any attention.

'Give us a chance to get something to eat first, can't you?' Rita said laughingly. She took off her hat and smiled at herself in the mirror above the mantelpiece. It was a curious smile as though she were amused by what she saw. Then she smoothed back her thick black hair. 'I told Paschal to bring in whatever was going. I'm on the train since ten. The heating was off as usual. I'm frizzled.'

'A wonder you wouldn't send us a wire,' said Mrs Lomasney as Rita sat down and grabbed some bread and butter.

'Hadn't the cash,' said Rita.

'But what happened, Rita?' Kitty asked brightly.

'You'll hear it all in due course. Reverend Mother is bound to write and tell ye how I lost my character.'

'Wisha, what did you do to her, child?' asked her mother with amusement. She had been through all this before, with Hasty and Kitty, and she knew that God was very good and nothing much ever happened.

'Fellow that wanted to marry me,' said Rita. 'He was in his last year at college, and his mother didn't like me, so she got Reverend Mother to give me the push.'

'But what business is it of hers?' asked Nellie.

'None whatever, girl,' said Rita.

But Kitty looked suspiciously at her. Rita wasn't natural: there was something about her that was not in control. After all, this was her first real love affair, and Kitty could not believe that she had gone about it like anyone else.

'Still, you worked pretty fast,' she said.

'You'd have to work fast in that place,' said Rita. 'There was only one possible man in the whole place – the bank clerk. We used to call him "The One". I wasn't there a week when a nun ticked me off for riding on the pillion of his motor-bike.'

'And did you?' Kitty asked innocently.

'Fat chance I got!' said Rita. 'They did that to every teacher to give her the idea that she was well-watched. The unfortunates were scared out of their wits. I only met Tony Donoghue a fortnight ago. He was home with a breakdown.'

'Well, well, well!' said her mother without rancour. 'No wonder his poor mother was upset. A boy that's not left college yet! Couldn't ye wait till he was qualified anyway?'

'Not very well,' said Rita. 'He's going to be a priest.'

Kitty sat back with a superior grin. She had known it all the time. Of course, Rita couldn't do anything like other people. If it hadn't been a priest it would have been a married man or a Negro, and Rita would have shown off about it just the same.

'What's that you say?' her father asked, springing to his feet.

'All right, don't blame me!' Rita said hastily, beaming at him. 'It wasn't my fault. He said he didn't want to be a priest. His mother was driving him into it. That's why he had the breakdown.'

'Let me out of this before I have a breakdown myself,' said Hasty. 'I'm the one that should be the priest. If I was I wouldn't be saddled with a mad, distracted family the way I am.'

He stamped out of the room, and the girls laughed. The idea of their father as a priest appealed to them almost as much as the idea of him as a mother. But Mrs Lomasney did not laugh.

49

'Reverend Mother was perfectly right,' she said severely. 'As if it wasn't hard enough on the poor boys without girls like you throwing temptation in their way. I think you behaved very badly, Rita.'

'All right, if you say so,' Rita said shortly with a boyish shrug, and refused to talk any more about it.

After supper, she said she was tired and went to bed, and her mother and sisters sat on in the front room, discussing the scandal. Someone rang and Nellie opened the door.

'Hullo, Ned,' she said. 'I suppose you came up to congratulate us.'

'Hullo,' Ned said, smiling primly with closed lips. With a sort of automatic movement he took off his overcoat and hat and hung them on the rack. Then he emptied the pockets with the same thoroughness. He had not changed much. He was thin and pale, spectacled and clever, with the same precise and tranquil manner – 'like an old Persian cat', as Nellie said. He read too many books. In the last year or two something seemed to have happened to him. He did not go to Mass any longer. Not going to Mass struck all the Lomasneys as too damn clever. 'On what?' he added, having avoided any unnecessary precipitation.

'You didn't know who was here?'

'No,' he said, raising his brows mildly.

'Rita!'

'Oh!' The same tone. It was part of his cleverness not to be surprised at anything. It was as though he regarded any attempt to surprise him as an invasion of his privacy.

'She's after getting the sack for trying to run off with a priest,' said Nellie.

If she thought that would shake him she was badly mistaken. He tossed his head with a silent chuckle and went into the room, adjusting his pince-nez. For a fellow who was supposed to be in love with her, this was very peculiar behaviour, Nellie thought. He put his hands in his trousers pockets and stood on the hearth with his legs well apart.

'Isn't it awful, Ned?' Mrs Lomasney asked in her deep voice.

'Is it?' Ned purred, smiling.

'With a priest!' cried Nellie.

'Now, he wasn't a priest, Nellie,' Mrs Lomasney said severely. 'Don't be trying to make it worse.'

'Suppose you tell me what happened,' suggested Ned.

'But sure, when we don't know, Ned,' cried Mrs Lomasney. 'You know what that one is like in one of her sulky fits. Maybe she'll tell you. She's up in bed.'

'I may as well try,' said Ned.

Still with his hands in his pockets, he rolled after Mrs Lomasney up the thickly carpeted stairs to Rita's little bedroom at the top of the house. While Mrs Lomasney went in to see that her daughter was decent he paused to look out over the river and the lighted city behind it. Rita, wearing a pink dressing jacket, was lying with one arm under her head. By the bed was a table with a packet of cigarettes she had been using as an ashtray. He smiled and shook his head reprovingly.

'Hullo, Ned,' she said, reaching him a bare arm. 'Give us a kiss. I'm quite kissable now.'

He didn't need to be told that. He was astonished at the change in her. Her whole bony, boyish face seemed to have gone soft and mawkish and to be lit up from inside. He sat on an armchair by the bed, carefully pulling up the bottoms of his trousers, then put his hands in the pockets again and sat back with crossed legs.

'I suppose they're hopping downstairs,' said Rita.

'They seem a little excited,' Ned replied, with bowed head cocked sideways, looking like some wise old bird.

'Wait till they hear the details!' Rita said grimly.

'Are there details?' he asked mildly.

'Masses of them,' said Rita. 'Honest to God, Ned, I used to laugh at the glamour girls in the convent. I never knew you could get like that about a fellow. It's like something busting inside you. Cripes, I'm as soppy as a kid!'

'And what's the fellow like?' Ned asked curiously.

'Tony? How the hell do I know? He's decent enough, I suppose. His mother has a shop in the Main Street. He kissed me one night coming home and I was so furious I cut the socks off him. Next evening, he came round to apologize,

51

and I never got up or asked him to sit down or anything. I suppose I was still mad with him. He said he never slept a wink. "Didn't you?" said I. "It didn't trouble me much." Bloody lies, of course; I was twisting and turning the whole night. "I only did it because I was so fond of you," says he. "Is that what you told the last one, too?" said I. That got him into a wax as well, and he said I was calling him a liar. "And aren't you?" said I. Then I waited for him to hit me, but instead he began to cry, and then I began to cry – imagine me crying, Ned! – and the next thing I was sitting on his knee. Talk about the Babes in the Wood. First time he ever had a girl on his knee, he said, and you know how much of it I did.'

There was a discreet knock and Mrs Lomasney smiled benevolently at them round the door.

'I suppose 'tis tea Ned is having?' she asked in her deep voice.

'No, I'm having the tea,' Rita said lightly, throwing him a cigarette. 'Ned says he'd sooner a drop of the hard tack.'

'Oh, isn't that a great change, Ned?' cried Mrs Lomasney.

' 'Tis the shock,' said Rita. 'He didn't think I was that sort of girl.'

'He mustn't know much about girls,' said Mrs Lomasney.

'He's learning now,' said Rita.

When Paschal brought up the tray, Rita poured out tea for Ned and whiskey for herself. He made no comment: things like that were a commonplace in the Lomasney household.

'Anyway,' she went on, pulling at her cigarette, 'he told his old one he wanted to chuck the Church and marry me. There was ructions. The people in the shop at the other side of the street had a son a priest, and she wanted to be as good as them. Away with her up to Reverend Mother, and Reverend Mother sends for me. Did I want to destroy the young man and he on the threshold of a great calling? I told her 'twas his mother wanted to destroy him, and I asked her what sort of a priest did she think Tony would make. Oh, he'd be twice the man, after a sacrifice like that. Honest to God, Ned, the way that woman went on, you'd think she was talking of doctoring an old tom-cat. I think this damn country must be full of female vets. After that, she dropped the Holy Willie stuff and told me his mother was after getting into debt to put him in for the priesthood, and if he chucked it now, she'd never be able to pay it back. Wouldn't they kill you with style?'

'And what did you do then?'

'I went to see his mother, of course.'

'You didn't!'

'I told you I was off my head. I thought I might work it with the personal touch.'

'You don't seem to have been successful.'

'I'd as soon try the personal touch on a traction engine, Ned,' Rita said ruefully. 'That woman was twice my weight. I told her I wanted to marry Tony. "I'm sorry, you can't," she said. "What's to stop me?" says I. "He's gone too far," says she. "If he was gone further it wouldn't stop me," says I. I told her then what Reverend Mother said about the three hundred pounds and offered to pay it back for her if she let me marry him.'

'And had you the three hundred?' Ned asked in surprise.

'Ah, where would I get three hundred? And she knew it, the old jade! She didn't believe a word I said. I saw Tony afterwards, and he was crying. He said he didn't want to break her heart. I declare to God, Ned, that woman has as much heart as a traction engine.'

'Well, you seem to have done it in style,' said Ned as he put away his teacup.

'That wasn't the half of it. When I heard the difficulties his mother was making, I offered to live with him instead.'

'Live with him!' said Ned. That startled even him.

'Well, go away on holidays with him. Lots of girls do it. I know they do. And, God Almighty, isn't it only natural?'

'And what did he say to that?' Ned asked curiously.

'He was scared stiff.'

'He would be,' said Ned, giving his superior little sniff as he took out a packet of cigarettes.

'Oh, it's all very well for you,' cried Rita, bridling up.

'You may think you're a great fellow, all because you read Tolstoy and don't go to Mass, but you'd be just as scared if a doll offered to go to bed with you.'

'Try me,' he said sedately as he lit her cigarette, but somehow the idea of suggesting such a thing to Ned only made her laugh.

He stayed till quite late, and when he went downstairs Mrs Lomasney and the girls fell on him and dragged him into the sitting room.

'Well, doctor, how's the patient?' asked Mrs Lomasney.

'Oh, I think the patient is coming round nicely,' said Ned with a smile.

'But would you ever believe it, Ned?' she cried. 'A girl that wouldn't look at the side of the road a fellow was on, unless 'twas to go robbing orchards with him. You'll have another drop of whiskey?'

'I won't.'

'And is that all you're going to tell us?'

'You'll hear it all from herself.'

'We won't.'

'I dare say not,' he said with a hearty chuckle, and went for his coat.

'Wisha, Ned, what will your mother say when she hears it?' asked Mrs Lomasney, and Ned put his nose in the air and gave an exaggerated version of what Mrs Lomasney called 'his Hayfield sniff'.

' "All *quite* mad," ' he said.

'The dear knows, she might be right,' she said with resignation, helping him on with his coat. 'I hope your mother doesn't notice the smell of whiskey from your breath,' she added dryly just to show him that she missed nothing, and then stood at the door, looking up and down, while she waited for him to wave from the gate.

'Ah, with the help of God it might be all for the best,' she said as she closed the door behind him.

'If you think he's going to marry her, you're mistaken,' said Kitty. 'Merciful God, I'd like to see myself telling Bill O'Donnell a thing like that. He'd have my sacred life. That fellow positively enjoys it.'

'Ah, God is good,' her mother said cheerfully, kicking a mat into place. 'Some men might like that.'

Three

Ned apparently did, but he was the only one. Within a week, Kitty and Nellie were sick to death of Rita round the house. She was bad enough at the best of times – or so they said – but now she brooded and mooned and quarrelled. Most afternoons she strolled down the Dyke to Ned's little shop where she sat on the counter, swinging her legs and smoking, while Ned leaned against the window, tinkering with some delicate instrument at the insides of a watch. Nothing seemed to rattle Ned, not even Rita doing what no customer would dare to do. When he finished work he changed his coat and they went out to tea. He sat in a corner at the back of the teashop, pulled up the bottoms of his trousers, and took out a packet of cigarettes and a box of matches, which he placed on the table before him with a look that commanded them to stay there and not get lost. His face was pale and clear and bright, like an evening sky when the last light has drained from it.

'Anything wrong?' he asked one evening when she was moodier than usual.

'Oh, just fed up,' she said thrusting out her jaw.

'Still fretting?' he asked in surprise.

'Ah, no. I can get over that. It's Kitty and Nellie. They're bitches, Ned; proper bitches. And all because I don't wear my heart on my sleeve. If one of them got dumped by a fellow she'd take two aspirins and go to bed with the other one. They'd have a lovely talk – can't you imagine? "And was it then he said he loved you?" That sort of balls! I can't do it. And it's all because they're not sincere, Ned. They couldn't be sincere.'

'Remember, they have a long start on you,' Ned said.

'Is that it?' she asked without interest. 'They think I'm batty. Do you, Ned?'

'Not altogether,' he said with a tight-lipped smile. 'I've no

55

doubt that Mrs Donoghue, if that's her name, thought something of the sort.'

'And wasn't she right?' Rita asked tensely. 'Suppose she'd agreed to take the three hundred quid, wouldn't I be properly shown up? I wake in a sweat whenever I think of it. I'm just a bloody chancer, Ned. Where would I get three hundred quid?'

'Oh, I dare say someone would have lent it to you,' he said with a shrug.

'They would like hell. Would you?'

'Probably,' he said gravely after a moment's thought. 'I think I could raise it.'

'Are you serious?' she whispered earnestly.

'Quite,' he said in the same tone.

'Cripes, you must be very fond of me,' she gasped.

'Looks like it,' said Ned, and this time he laughed with real heartiness; a boy's laugh of sheer delight at her astonishment. Of course, it was just like Rita to regard a lifetime's friendship as sport, and the offer of three hundred pounds as the real thing.

'Would you marry me?' she asked with a frown. 'I'm not proposing to you, mind, only asking,' she added hastily.

'Certainly, whenever you like,' he said, spreading his hands.

'Honest to God?'

'Cut my throat,' he replied, making the schoolboy gesture.

'My God, why didn't you ask me before I went down to that kip? I'd have married you like a shot. Was it the way you weren't keen on me?' she added, wondering if there wasn't really something queer about him, as her sisters said.

'No,' he replied matter-of-factly, drawing himself together like an old clock preparing to strike. 'I think I've been keen on you since the first day I met you.'

'It's easily seen you're a Neddy Ned,' she said. 'I go after mine with a scalping knife.'

'I stalk mine,' he said smugly.

'Cripes, Ned,' she said with real regret, 'I wish you'd told me sooner. I couldn't marry you now.'

'Couldn't you? Why not?'

'Because it wouldn't be fair to you.'

'You think I can't look after myself?'

'I have to look after you now.' She glanced round the restaurant to make sure that no one was listening, and then went on in a dry, dispassionate voice, leaning one elbow wearily on the table. 'I suppose you'll think this is all cod, but it's not. Honest to God, I think you're the finest bloody man I ever met – even though you do think you're an atheist or something,' she interjected maliciously with a character-istic Lomasney flourish in the cause of Faith and Father-land. 'There's no one in the world I have more respect for. I think I'd nearly cut my throat if I did something you really disapproved of – I don't mean telling lies or going on a skite,' she added hastily. 'That's only gas. I mean something that really shocked you. I think if I was tempted I'd ask myself : "How the hell would I face Lowry afterwards?" '

For a moment she thought from his smile that he was going to cry. Then he squelched the butt of his cigarette on a plate and spoke in an extraordinarily quiet voice.

'That'll do me grand for a beginning,' he said.

'It wouldn't, Ned,' she said sadly. 'That's why I say I have to look after you now. You couldn't understand it unless it happened to yourself and you fell in love with a doll the way I fell in love with Tony. Tony is a scut, and a cowardly scut at that, but I was cracked about him. If he came in here now and asked me to go off to Killarney on a weekend with him, I'd buy a nightdress and a toothbrush and go. And I wouldn't give a damn what you or anybody thought. I might chuck myself in the lake afterwards, but I'd go. Christ, Ned,' she exclaimed, flushing and looking as though she might burst into tears, 'he couldn't come into a room but I went all mushy inside. That's what the real thing is like.'

'Well,' said Ned, apparently not in the least put out – in fact, looking rather pleased with himself, Rita thought – 'I'm in no hurry. In case you get tired of scalping them, the offer will still be open.'

'Thanks, Ned,' she said absent-mindedly, as though she weren't listening.

While he paid the bill, she stood in the porch, doing her face in the big mirror that flanked it, and paying no attention to the crowds who were hurrying homeward through lighted streets. As she emerged from the shop she turned on him suddenly.

'About that matter, Ned,' she said. 'Will you ask me again, or do I have to ask you?'

He just managed to refrain from laughing outright.

'As you like,' he said with quiet amusement. 'Suppose I repeat the proposal every six months.'

'That would be a hell of a time to wait if I changed my mind,' she said with a scowl. 'All right,' she added, taking his arm. 'I know you well enough to ask you. If you don't want me by that time, you can always say so. I won't mind. I'm used to it now.'

Four

Ned's proposal came as a considerable support to Rita. It buttressed her self-esteem, which was always in danger of collapsing. She might be ugly and uneducated and a bit of a chancer, but the best man in Cork – the best in Ireland, she sometimes thought – wanted to marry her, even when she had been let down by another man. That was a queer one for her enemies! So while Kitty and Nellie made fun of her, she bided her time, waiting till she could really rock them. Since her childhood she had never given anything away without squeezing the last ounce of theatrical effect from it. She would tell her sisters, but not till she could make them feel properly sick.

It was a pity she didn't because Ned was not the only one. There was also Justin Sullivan, the lawyer, who had once been by way of being engaged to Nellie. He had not become engaged to her because Nellie was as slippery as an eel, and had her cap set all the time at a solicitor called Fahy whom Justin despised with his whole heart and soul as a light-headed, butterfly sort of man. But Justin continued to come to the house. There happened to be no other that suited him half as well, and besides, he knew that sooner or later Nellie would make a mess of her life with Fahy, and his services would be required.

Justin, in fact, was a sticker. He was a good deal older than Rita; a tall, burly man with a broad face, a brow that was rising from baldness as well as brains, and a slow, watchful, ironic air. Like many lawyers he tended to conduct a conversation as though the person he was speaking to was a hostile witness who had to be coaxed into an admission of perjury or bullied into one of mental deficiency.

When Justin began to talk Fahy simply clutched his head and retired to sit on the stairs. 'Can no one shut that fellow up?' he would moan with a martyred air. No one could. The girls shot their little darts at him, but he only brushed them aside. Ned was the only one who could even stand up to him, and when the two of them argued about religion, the room became a desert. Justin, of course, was all for the Church. 'Imagine for a moment that I am Pope,' he would declaim in a throaty, rounded voice that turned easily to pompousness. 'Easiest thing in the world, Justin,' Kitty assured him once. He drank whiskey like water, and the more he drank, the more massive and logical and piously Catholic he became.

But for all his truculent airs he was exceedingly gentle, patient and understanding, and disliked the way her sisters ragged Rita.

'Tell me, Nellie,' he asked one night in his lazy, amiable way, 'do you talk like that to Rita because you like it, or out of a sense of duty?'

'How soft you have it!' cried Nellie. 'We have to live with her. You haven't.'

'That may be my misfortune, Nellie,' said Justin.

'Is that a proposal, Justin?' Kitty asked shrewdly.

'Scarcely, Kitty,' said Justin. 'You're not what I might call a good jury.'

'Better be careful or you'll have her calling on your mother, Justin,' Kitty said maliciously.

'I hope my mother has sufficient sense to realize it would be an honour, Kitty,' Justin said severely.

When he rose to go, Rita accompanied him to the hall.

'Thanks for the moral support, Justin,' she said in a low voice and threw an overcoat over her shoulders to accompany him to the gate. When he opened the door they both stood and gazed round them. It was a moonlit night: the garden, patterned in black and silver, sloped to the quiet suburban roadway where the gas lamps burned with a dim green light. Beyond this gateways shaded by black trees led to flights of steps or steep-sloping avenues behind the moonlit houses on the river's edge.

'God, isn't it lovely?' said Rita.

'Oh, by the way, Rita, that was a proposal,' he said, slipping his arm through hers.

'Janey Mack, they're falling,' she said, and gave his arm a squeeze.

'What are?'

'Proposals. I never knew I was so popular.'

'Why? Have you had others?'

'I had one anyway.'

'And did you accept it?'

'No,' Rita said doubtfully. 'Not quite. At least, I don't think I did.'

'You might consider this one,' Justin said with unusual humility. 'You know, of course, that I was very fond of Nellie. At one time I was very fond of her, indeed. You don't mind that, I hope. It's all over and done with now, and no regrets on either side.'

'No, Justin, of course I don't mind. If I felt like marrying you I wouldn't give it a second thought. But I was very much in love with Tony too, and that's not all over and done with yet.'

'I know that, Rita,' he said gently. 'I know exactly what you feel. We've all been through it.' He might as well have left it there, but, being a lawyer, Justin liked to see his case properly set out. 'That won't last forever. In a month or two you'll be over it, and then you'll wonder what you saw in that fellow.'

'I don't think so, Justin,' she said with a crooked smile, not altogether displeased to be able to enlighten him about the utter hopelessness of her position. 'I think it will take a great deal longer than that.'

'Well, say six months even,' Justin went on, prepared to yield a point to the defence. 'All I ask is that in one month or six, when you've got over your regrets for this – this amiable young man,' (momentarily his voice took on its familiar ironic tone) 'you'll give me a thought. I'm old enough not to make any more mistakes. I know I'm fond of you, and I feel sure I could make a success of my end of it.'

'What you really mean is that I wasn't in love with Tony at all,' Rita said, keeping her temper with the greatest difficulty. 'Isn't that it?'

'Not quite,' Justin replied judiciously. Even if he had had a serenade as well as moonlight and a girl, Justin could not have resisted correcting what he considered a false deduction. 'I've no doubt you were very much attracted by this – this clerical Adonis; this Mr Whatever-his-name-is, or that at any rate you thought you were, which in practice comes to the same thing, but I also know that that sort of thing, though it's painful enough while it lasts, doesn't last very long.'

'You mean yours didn't, Justin,' Rita said tartly. By this time she was flaming.

'I mean mine or anyone else's,' said Justin. 'Because love – the only sort of thing you can really call love – is something that comes with experience. You're probably too young yet to know what the real thing is.'

As Rita had only recently told Ned that he didn't yet know what the real thing was, she found this very hard to stomach.

'How old would you say you'd have to be,' she asked viciously. 'Thirty-five?'

'You'll know soon enough – when it hits you,' said Justin.

'Honest to God, Justin,' she said withdrawing her arm and looking at him furiously, 'I think you're the thickest man I ever met.'

'Goodnight, my dear,' said Justin with perfect good humour, and he took the few steps to the gate at a run.

Rita stood gazing after him with folded arms. At the age

of twenty to be told that there is anything you don't know about love is like a knife in your heart.

Five

Kitty and Nellie persuaded Mrs Lomasney that the best way of distracting Rita's mind was to find her a new job. As a new environment was also supposed to be good for her complaint, Mrs Lomasney wrote to her sister, who was a nun in England, and the sister found her work in a convent there. Rita let on to be indifferent though she complained bitterly enough to Ned.

'But why England?' he asked in surprise.

'Why not?'

'Wouldn't any place nearer do you?'

'I suppose I wouldn't be far enough away.'

'But why not make up your own mind?'

'I'll probably do that too,' she said with a short laugh. 'I'd like to see what's in theirs first though. I might have a surprise for them.'

She certainly had that. She was to leave for England on Friday, and on Wednesday the girls gave a farewell party. Wednesday was the weekly half-holiday, and it rained steadily all day. The girls' friends all turned up. Most of these were men: Bill O'Donnell of the bank, who was engaged to Kitty; Fahy, the solicitor, who was Justin's successful rival for Nellie; Justin himself, who simply could not be kept out of the house by anything short of an injunction, Ned Lowry and a few others. Hasty soon retired with his wife to the dining room to read the evening paper. He said all his daughters' young men looked exactly alike and he never knew which of them he was talking to.

Bill O'Donnell was acting as barman. He was a big man, bigger even that Justin, with a battered boxer's face and a Negro smile that seemed to well up from the depths of good humour with life rather than from anything that happened in it. He carried out loud conversations with everyone he poured out a drink for, and his voice overrode every intervening tête-à-tête, and even challenged the piano, on which Nellie was vamping music-hall songs.

'Who's this one for, Rita?' he asked. 'A bottle of Bass for Paddy. Ah, the stout man! Remember the New Year's Night in Bandon, Paddy? Remember how you had to carry me up to the bank in evening dress and jack me up between the two wings of the desk? Kitty, did I ever tell you about that night in Bandon?'

'Once a week for the past five years, Bill,' Kitty sang out cheerfully.

'Nellie,' said Rita. 'I think it's time for Bill to sing his song. *Let Me Like a Soldier Fall*, Bill!'

'My one little song!' Bill said with a roar of laughter. 'The only song I know, but I sing it grand. Don't I, Nellie? Don't I sing it fine?'

'Fine!' agreed Nellie, looking up at his big moon-face beaming at her over the piano. 'As the man said to my mother, "Finest bloody soprano I ever heard."'

'He did not, Nellie,' Bill said sadly. 'You're making that up ... Silence, please!' he shouted, clapping his hands. 'Ladies and gentlemen, I must apologize. I ought to sing something like Tosti's *Goodbye* but the fact is, ladies and gentlemen, that I don't know Tosti's *Goodbye*.'

'Recite it, Bill,' suggested Justin amiably.

'I don't know the words of it either, Justin,' said Bill. 'In fact, I'm not sure if there is any such song, but if there is, I ought to sing it.'

'Why, Bill?' asked Rita innocently. She was wearing a long black dress that threw up the unusual brightness of her dark, bony face. She looked more cheerful than she had looked for months. All the evening it was as though she were laughing to herself at something.

'Because 'twould be only right, Rita,' Bill said with great melancholy, putting his arm round her and drawing her closer. 'You know I'm very fond of you, don't you, Rita?'

'And I'm mad about you, Bill,' Rita said candidly.

'I know that, Rita,' he said mournfully, pulling at his collar as though to give himself air. 'I only wish you weren't going, Rita. This place isn't the same without you. Kitty won't mind my saying that,' he added with a nervous glance at Kitty, who was flirting with Justin on the sofa.

'Are you going to sing your blooming old song or not?' Nellie asked impatiently, running her fingers over the keys.

'I'm going to sing now in one minute, Nellie,' Bill replied ecstatically, stroking Rita fondly under the chin. 'I only want Rita to know we'll miss her.'

'Damn it, Bill,' Rita said, snuggling up to him, 'if you go on like that I won't go at all. Would you sooner I didn't go?'

'I would sooner it, Rita, he said, stroking her cheeks and eyes. 'You're too good for the fellows there.'

'Oh, go on doing that, Bill,' she said. 'It's gorgeous, and you're making Kitty mad jealous.'

'Kitty isn't jealous,' Bill said mawkishly. 'Kitty is a lovely girl and you're a lovely girl. I hate to see you go, Rita.'

'That settles it, Bill,' she said, pulling herself free of him with a mock-determined air. 'As you feel that way about it, I won't go at all.'

'Won't you though!' said Kitty sweetly.

'Don't worry your head about it, Bill,' said Rita briskly. 'It's all off.'

Justin, who had been quietly getting through large whiskies, looked up lazily.

'Perhaps I should have mentioned that the young lady has just done me the honour of proposing to me, and I've accepted her,' he boomed.

Ned, who had been enjoying the little scene between Bill and Rita, looked at Justin in surprise.

'Bravo! Bravo!' cried Bill, clapping his hands with delight. 'A marriage has been arranged and all the rest of it – what? I must give you a kiss, Rita. Justin, you don't mind if I give Rita a kiss?'

'Not at all, not at all,' said Justin with a lordly wave of the hand. 'Anything that's mine is yours.'

'You're not serious, Justin, are you?' Kitty asked incredulously.

'Oh, I'm serious all right,' said Justin, and then he gave Rita a puzzled look. 'I'm not quite certain whether your sister is. Are you, Rita?'

'What?' Rita asked, as though she were listening to something else.

'Why? Are you trying to give me the push already?' asked Justin with amusement.

'We're much obliged for the information,' Nellie said angrily as she rose from the piano. 'I wonder did you tell Father?'

'Hardly,' said Rita coolly. 'It was only settled an hour ago.'

'Maybe 'twill do with some more settling by the time Father is done with you,' Nellie said furiously. 'The impudence of you! Go in at once and tell him.'

'Keep your hair on, girl,' Rita said with cool malice and then went jauntily out of the room. Kitty and Nellie began to squabble viciously with Justin. They were convinced that the whole scene had been arranged by Rita to make them look ridiculous, and in this they weren't very far out. Justin sat back and began to enjoy the sport. Then Ned struck a match and lit another cigarette, and something about the slow, careful way he did it drew everyone's attention. Just because he was not the sort to make a fuss, anything unusual about him stuck out, and a feeling of awkwardness ensued. Ned was too old a friend for the girls not to feel that way about him.

Rita returned, laughing.

'Consent refused,' she growled, bowing her head and tugging the wrong side of an imaginary moustache.

'What did I tell you?' Nellie said without rancour.

'You don't think it makes any difference?' asked Rita dryly.

'What did he say?' asked Kitty.

'Oh, he hadn't a notion who I was talking about,' Rita said lightly. ' "Justin who?" ' she mimicked. ' "How the hell do you think I can remember all the young scuts ye bring to the house?" '

'Was he mad?' asked Kitty.

'Hopping. The poor man can't even settle down to read his *Echo* without one of his daughters interrupting him to announce her engagement.'

'He didn't call us scuts?' Bill asked in a tone of genuine grief.

'Oh, begor, that was the very word he used, Bill.'

'Did you tell him he was very fond of me the day I gave him the tip for Golden Boy at the Park Races?' asked Justin.

'I did,' said Rita. 'I told him you were the stout block of a fellow with the brown hair that he said had the fine intelligence, and he said he never gave a damn about intelligence. Character was all that mattered. He wanted me to marry the thin fellow with the specs. "Only bloody gentleman that comes to this house." '

'Is it Ned?' asked Nellie.

'Of course. I asked him why he didn't tell me that before and he nearly ate the head off me. "Jesus Christ, girl, don't I feed and clothe ye? Isn't that enough without having to coort for ye as well. Next thing is ye'll be asking me to have a couple of babies for ye." Anyway, Ned,' she added with a crooked, almost malicious smile, 'there's no doubt about who was Pa's favourite.'

Once more the attention was directed on Ned. He put his cigarette down with care and rose, holding out his hand.

'I wish you all the luck in the world, Justin,' he said.

'I know that well, Ned,' boomed Justin catching Ned's hand. 'And I'd feel the same if it was you.'

'And you too, Miss Lomasney,' Ned said gaily.

'Thanks, Mr Lowry,' she replied with the same crooked smile.

And they all felt afterwards as though they had been attending a funeral.

Six

Justin and Rita married, and Ned, like all the Hayfield Hourigans, behaved in a decorous and sensible manner. He did not take to drink or violence or do any of the things people are expected to do under the circumstances. He gave them an expensive clock as a wedding present, went a couple of times to visit them, permitted Justin to try and convert him back to Catholicism, and took Rita to the pictures when Justin was on circuit. At the same time he began to walk out with an assistant in Halpin's; a gentle, humorous girl with a great mass of jet-black hair, a snub nose and a long, melancholy face. You saw them everywhere together. He also went regularly to Sunday's Well to see the old couple and Nellie, who wasn't married yet. One evening when he called, Mr and Mrs Lomasney were down at the church, but Rita was there, Justin being again away. It was months since she and Ned had met; she was having a baby and very near her time, and it made her self-conscious and rude. She said it made her feel like a yacht that had been turned into a cargo-boat. Three or four times she said things to Ned that would have maddened anyone else, but he took them in his usual way, without resentment.

'And how's little Miss Bitch?' she asked insolently.

'Little Miss who?' he asked.

'Miss – how the hell can I remember the names of all your dolls? The Spanish-looking one who sells the knickers at Halpin's.'

'Oh, she's very well, thanks.'

'What you might call a prudent marriage,' Rita went on, all on edge.

'How's that?'

'You'll have the ring and the trousseau at cost price.'

'Aren't you very interested in her?' Nellie asked suspiciously.

'I don't give a damn about her,' Rita said contemptuously. 'Would Senorita What's-her-name ever let you stand godfather to my footballer, Ned?'

'Why not?' Ned asked mildly. 'I'd be delighted, of course.'

'You have the devil's own neck to ask him after the way you treated him,' said Nellie.

Nellie was fascinated. She knew that Rita was in one of her emotional states and longed to know what it all meant. Ordinarily Rita would have delighted in thwarting her, but now it was as though she actually wanted an audience.

'What did I do to him?' she asked with interest.

'Codding him along like that for years, and then marrying a man that was twice your age. What sort of conduct is that?'

'Well, how did he expect me to know the difference?'

Ned rose, and took out a packet of cigarettes. Like Nellie, he knew that Rita had deliberately staged the scene for some purpose of her own. She was leaning far back in her chair and laughed up at him while she took a cigarette and waited for him to light it.

'Come on, Rita,' he said encouragingly. 'As you've said so much you may as well tell us the rest.'

'What else is there to tell?'

'What had you against me,' he said, growing pale.

'Who said I had anything against you?'

'Didn't you?'

'Not a damn thing. Just that I didn't love you. Didn't I tell you distinctly when you asked me to marry you that I didn't love you? I suppose you thought I didn't mean it?'

He paused for a moment and then raised his eyebrows.

'I did,' he said quietly.

She laughed. Nellie did not laugh.

'The conceit of some people!' Rita said lightly: then, with a change of tone: 'I had nothing against you, Ned. This was the one I had the needle in. Herself and Kitty forcing me into it.'

'Well, the impudence of you!' cried Nellie.

'And isn't it true for me? Weren't you both trying to get me out of the house?'

'We were not,' Nellie replied hotly. 'And even if we were, that has nothing to do with it. We didn't want you to marry Justin if you wanted to marry Ned.'

'I didn't want to marry Ned. I didn't want to marry at all.'

'What made you change your mind, so?'

'Nothing made me change my mind. I didn't care about anyone only Tony, only I didn't want to go to that damn place, and I had no alternative. I had to marry one of them, so I made up my mind that I'd marry the first one that called.'

It was directed to Nellie, but every word was aimed straight at Ned, and Nellie was wise enough to realize it.

'My God, you must have been mad!' she said.

'I felt it,' Rita said with a shrug. 'I sat at the window the whole afternoon, looking out at the rain. Remember that day, Ned?'

He nodded.

'Blame the rain if you want to blame something. I think I half hoped you'd come first. Justin came instead – an old aunt of his was sick and he came to supper. I saw him at the gate and he waved to me with his old brolly. I ran downstairs to open the door for him. "Justin, if you still want to marry me, I'm ready," I said, and I grabbed him by the coat. He gave me a dirty look – you know Justin! "Young woman, there's a time and place for everything," he said, and off with him to the lavatory. Talk about romantic engagements! Damn the old kiss did I get off him, even!'

'I declare to God!' Nellie said in stupefaction. 'You're not natural, Rita.'

'I know,' Rita said, laughing again at her own irresponsibility. 'Cripes, when I knew what I'd done I nearly dropped dead!'

'Oh, so you did come to your senses, for once?' Nellie asked.

'Of course I did. That's the trouble with Justin. He's always right. That fellow knew I wouldn't be married a week before I'd forgotten Tony. And there was I, sure that my life was over and that it was marriage or the river. Women!' she cried, shaking her head in a frenzy. 'Good God. The idiots we make of ourselves about men!'

'And I suppose it was then that you found out you'd married the wrong man?' Nellie asked, but not inquisitively this time. She knew.

'Who said I married the wrong man?' Rita asked hotly.

'It sounds damn like it, Rita,' Nellie said wearily.

'You get things all wrong, Nellie,' Rita said, her teeth on edge again. 'You jump to conclusions too much. If I married the wrong man, I wouldn't be likely to tell you – or Ned either.'

She looked mockingly at Ned, but her look belied her. It was plain enough now why she needed Nellie as audience. It kept her from saying more than she had to say, from saying things that once said, might make her own life unbearable. We all do it. Once let her say 'Ned, I love you', which was all she was saying, and he would have to do something about it, and then everything would fall in ruin about them.

He rose and flicked his cigarette ash into the fire. Then he stood with his back to it, his hands behind his back, his feet spread out on the hearth, exactly as he had stood on that night when he had defended her against her family.

'You mean, if I'd come earlier you'd have married me?' he asked quietly.

'If you'd come earlier, I'd probably be asking Justin to stand godfather to your brat,' said Rita. 'And how do you know but Justin would be walking out the Senorita, Ned?'

'And you wouldn't be quite so interested whether he was or not,' Nellie said, but she didn't say it maliciously. It was only too plain what Rita meant, and Nellie was sorry for her. She had a long lifetime yet to go through. 'Dear God,' she added ingenuously, 'isn't life awful?'

Ned turned and lashed his cigarette savagely into the fire. Rita looked up at him mockingly.

'Go on' she taunted him. 'Say it, blast you!'

'I couldn't,' he said bitterly.

A month later, he married the Senorita.

Crab Apple Jelly (1944)

THE CUSTOM OF THE COUNTRY

One

It is remarkable the difference that even one foreigner can make in a community when he is not yet accustomed to its ways, the way he can isolate its customs and hold them up for your inspection. Things that had been as natural to you as bread suddenly need to be explained, and the really maddening thing is that you can't explain them. After a while you begin to wonder if they're real at all. Sometimes you doubt if you're real yourself.

We saw that with the new factory when they brought over an English foreman named Ernest Thompson to teach the local workers the job. It was not that people didn't like Ernie. They did. He was a thoroughly obliging chap, more particularly in confidential matters that our people wouldn't like to discuss among themselves, and a number of respectable married couples, as well as some that were neither married nor respectable, were under obligations to him which they would have found it dangerous to admit. Nor was it that he was stand-offish, because, in fact, he wanted to be in on everything, from the way you made love to your wife to the way the mountainy men made poteen, and he was never without ideas for improving the one or the other. There wasn't much he didn't know something about, and quite a lot of things he let on to know everything about. But for all that he could give you useful tips about mending a car or building a house, he put you off at the same time by the feeling that if he was natural, then there must be something wrong with you.

Take, for instance, the time when he started walking out with Anna Martin. Anna was a really nice girl even if she was a bit innocent. That is never much harm in a girl you care for. Anna's innocence showed even in her face, plump, dark, childish, and all in smooth curves from the bulging boyish forehead to the big, dimpled chin, with the features nesting in the hollows as if only waiting for a patch of sunlight to emerge.

Her mother, a widow woman of good family who had had the misfortune to marry one Willie Martin, a man of no class, kept a tiny huckster shop at a corner of the Cross. She was a nice, well-preserved, well-spoken little roly-poly of a woman with bad feet which gave her a waddle, and piles, which made her sit on a high hard chair, and she sat for the greater part of the day in the kitchen behind the shop with her hands joined in her lap and an air of regret for putting the world to the trouble of knowing her, though all the time she was thinking complacently of the past glories of her family, the Henebry-Hayeses of Coolnaleama. Mrs Martin had a sallow face that looked very innocent down the middle and full of guile round the edges, like a badly ironed pillowcase, and appeared so refined and ethereal that you thought her soul must be made of shot silk. Anna knew her mother's soul was made of stouter stuff. She was a woman of great principle, and if Anna bought a dress in a fashionable Protestant shop, she had to pretend it was bought in a Catholic one. It was not that her mother would create scenes; she was not a woman for scenes, but back the Protestant frock would go if she had to bring it herself. The coffee they drank tasted mouldy, but it was Catholic coffee. She didn't believe in digging with the wrong foot; it was linked somewhere in her mind with family pride and keeping to your own class, and until the last maid left, having smashed the last bit of family china off the kitchen wall, and denounced 'the Hungry Hayeses' as she called them, to the seventh generation of horse-stealers and land-grabbers, Mrs Martin had never ceased in her humble deprecating way to persuade them to wear cap and apron, serve from the left, and call Anna 'miss'.

That she had failed was entirely the doing of the Mahoneys, two mad sisters who kept another small shop farther up towards the chapel and corrupted their maids with tea and scandal. They were two tall, excitable women, one with the face of a cow and the other with the face of a greyhound, and the greyhound had a son who was going in for the priesthood. The madness of the Mahoneys took a peculiar form which made them think themselves as good as the Henebry-Hayeses of Coolnaleama; a harmless enough illusion in itself if only they didn't act as though it were true. When Mrs Martin had Anna taught to play the violin, they had Jerry taught to play the piano (the scandal was dreadful, because the piano wouldn't go through their front door and up the stairs, and had to be hoisted aboard like a cow on a hooker). When Anna and Jerry were both to have played at a concert in the convent, the Mahoneys, by a diabolical intrigue, succeeded in getting her name omitted from the programme, and Mrs Martin refused to let Anna play at all and dragged her from the hall by the hand. Sister Angela, Mrs Martin's friend, agreed that she was perfectly right, but Anna bawled the whole night through and said her mother had made a show of her. Even at that age Anna had no sense of what was fitting.

Then Jeremiah Henebry-Hayes, Mrs Martin's brother, came home from the States and stayed with her, driving off each day to Killarney, Blarney, or Glengariff in a big car with the Stars and Stripes flying from the bonnet, and the madness of the Mahoneys reached such a pitch that they brought home a dissolute brother of their own from Liverpool and hired a car for him to drive round in. They couldn't get rid of him after, and it was Mrs Martin who gave him the couple of cigarettes on tick. She was never paid, but it was worth it to her.

It was no easy life she had of it at all, with the Mahoneys sending in their spies to see if she was selling proprietary stuff at cut prices, but it must be said for the commercial travellers that they knew a lady when they saw one, and tipped her off about the Mahoneys' manoeuvres.

Finally Ernest Thompson made the shop his home. Mrs Martin's cooking was good, and he returned the compliment in scores of ways from mending the electric light to finding cures for her piles. She couldn't get over his referring to the piles, but, of course, he wasn't Irish. She was very amiable with him, and waddled round after Anna, correcting her constantly over her shoulder in a refined and humorous way; not, as Anna well knew, in any hope of improving her, but just to show Ernest that she knew what was becoming.

'Well, well!' she exclaimed in mock alarm at one of Anna's outbursts of commonness. 'Where on earth do you pick up those horrible expressions. Anna? I wonder do young ladies in England talk like that, Mr Thompson?'

'I should say there aren't many young ladies anywhere who can talk like Anna,' Ernest said fondly.

'Oh, my!' cried Mrs Martin, deliberately misunderstanding him and throwing up her hands in affected fright. 'You don't mean she's as bad as that, Mr Thompson?'

'Anna is a very exceptional girl, Mrs Martin,' he replied gravely.

'Ah, I don't know,' sighed Mrs Martin, looking doubtfully at Anna as though she were some sort of beast she wouldn't like to pass off on a friend. 'Of course, she should be all right,' she added, ironing out another crease or two in the middle of her face. 'She comes of good stock, on one side anyway. I don't suppose you'd have heard of the Henebry-Hayeses?' she added with quivering modesty. 'You wouldn't, to be sure – how could you?'

Ernest skirted this question, which seemed to involve a social gaffe of the first order, like not knowing who the Habsburgs were.

'Of course,' Mrs Martin went on, almost going in convulsions of abnegation, 'I believe people nowadays don't think as much of breeding as they used to, but I'm afraid I'm terribly old-fashioned.'

'You're not old-fashioned at all, Ma,' said Anna, who knew all the vanity that her mother concealed behind her girlish modesty. 'You're antediluvian.'

'Of course, her father's people were what we in Ireland call self-made,' added Mrs Martin, revenging herself in a ladylike way. 'I suppose you can see it breaking out in her sometimes.'

On the whole, though Mrs Martin wasn't an enthusiastic woman, she was inclined to approve of Ernest. At any rate he was socially more presentable than an Irishman of the same class. Only a woman as refined as herself would be likely to notice that he wasn't quite the thing. That showed how little Mrs Martin really knew about people; Ernest wasn't the thing at all for even while he was listening deferentially to her account of the Henebry-Hayeses, he was plotting in connexion with Anna things that would have made the Henebry-Hayeses turn in their graves. Ernest was lonely, he was accustomed to having women; he knew all the approaches. He took Anna for drives, filled her with gin, talked to her in the most intimate fashion of his experiences with other women, but he found that he was really getting nowhere with her. Anna's innocence would have stopped a cavalry charge.

She didn't even understand what he was getting at until one night when the two of them were walking in a lane up the hill with the valley of the city far below them. Ernest felt if Anna had any romance in her at all that this should touch her. He suggested that they go away for a weekend together.

'But what do you want to go away for a weekend for, Ernie?' drawled Anna in an accent which her mother said was like the wind up a flue.

'Because I want to make love to you, Anna,' he replied in a voice that throbbed like an organ.

'And what do you think you're doing now?' Anna asked gaily.

'Don't you want me to make love to you?' he asked earnestly, seizing her by the wrists and looking deep into her eyes. 'We love one another, don't we? What more do we need?'

'Ah, merciful God, Ernie' she cried in panic, understanding him at last. 'I couldn't do that. I couldn't.'

'Why not, Anna?' He was almost sobbing.

'Because 'twould be a sin.'

'Is love like ours a sin?'

'What the hell has love to do with it? 'Tis always a sin unless people are married.'

'Always?'

75

'Always.'

He looked at her doubtfully for a few moments as though he were trying to hypnotize her and then dropped her hands mournfully and with finality.

'Oh, well, if you feel like that about it!'

She saw he had expected something different and that he was now disappointed and hurt. She took out her cigarettes and offered him one, more by way of peace-offering than anything else. By way of peace-offering, he also refused it. She saw then he was really mad with her. He stood against the wall, his hands by his sides, looking up at the sky, and the match-flame showed his plump, dark, handsome face with the injured expression of a child who has been told he can't have an apple. Anna felt terrible about it.

'I suppose you think I'm not fond of you now?' she drawled miserably, turning up her face to let out a column of smoke.

'I don't go by what people think,' Ernest said stiffly without even looking at her. 'I can only go by how they behave.'

'Because I am, in case you want to know,' she said, trying to keep back her tears. 'And God knows, I wouldn't tell you a lie.'

'I suppose it's not altogether your fault,' Ernest said in the same stiff judicial tone. 'I dare say you're inhibited.'

'I dare say I am,' agreed Anna, who did not know what he was talking about, but was prepared to plead guilty to anything if only it made him happy. 'I suppose 'tis only the custom of the country. Would an English girl do it?'

'If she loved a man,' Ernest said hollowly, studying the Milky Way.

'And what would her family say?'

'They wouldn't be consulted,' Ernest said. 'A woman's life is her own, isn't it?'

It was as well for Mrs Martin that she couldn't hear that question. It was as well for Ernest that the dead generations of Henebry-Hayeses in Coolnaleama couldn't hear it, because men had died at their hands for less.

Two

In spite of this rebuff Ernest continued to call and see Anna. He borrowed a car and took her and her mother for long drives through the country. By this time Mrs Martin had become quite reconciled to the thought of him as a husband for Anna. So few Irishmen of good family would look at a girl without money; and if Anna had to marry outside what Mrs Martin regarded as her class, it was as well for her to marry a foreigner whose origins would be obscured by his manners.

'Of course, he's not what I'd call a gentleman,' she said with resignation. 'But then, I suppose we can't have everything.'

'Well, I'm not a lady either, so we suit one another fine,' retorted Anna.

'It's nice to hear it from your own lips anyway,' giggled her mother in that genteel way she had of bridling up.

'Well, I'm not and that's the holy bloody all of it,' said Anna, being deliberately coarse so as to persuade her mother that everything was fine. 'I'm not a lady, and I couldn't be a lady, and it's no use trying to make me a lady.'

'The language is absolutely delightful,' her mother said with the affected lightness that always drove Anna mad. 'I hope you talk to them like that in England. They're sure to love it.'

'Who said I was going to England anyway?' bawled Anna growing commoner under the provocation. 'He didn't ask me yet.'

'Well, I hope when he does that you won't forget you're supposed to be a Catholic as well as a lady,' said her mother, moving off as though to bed.

'A Catholic?' Anna cried in alarm. 'What difference does that make?'

'Oh, none in the world, child,' her mother said cheerfully over her shoulder. 'Only that you can't marry him unless he turns.'

'Oh, Christ!' moaned Anna.

'I beg your pardon, Anna,' her mother said, huffing up in the doorway, a picture of martyred gentility. 'Did I hear you say something?'

'I said I might as well stuff my head in the gas oven,' said Anna.

'Ah, well, I dare say he'll turn,' her mother said complacently, 'Most men do.'

But Anna, lying awake, could not treat it so lightly. Every morning she was up at seven, gave her mother tea in bed before going to early Mass, did the shopping, and minded the shop three nights a week, and a girl does not behave like that unless she has a man so much on her mind that whatever she does seems done under his eye, for his approval, as though she were living in a glasshouse. 'I have it bad all right,' she thought in her common way, but even her commonness seemed different when Ernest was there. She had been brought up to look on it as a liability, but Ernest made it seem like a talent.

Besides, she already had a bad conscience about the weekend she had denied him. Anna might be inhibited, but her maternal instinct was very strong, and she was haunted by the memory of Ernest, looking up at the stars on the point of tears, and all because of her; and she felt that, no matter what the priest said, it could never, never be right to deprive a man you cared for of any little pleasure he valued. To suggest now that she should refuse to marry him unless he became a Catholic seemed to her the end.

He did propose to her a fortnight later, when they were in the sitting room that overlooked the Cross – a stuffy little room with all the Henebry-Hayes treasures round them. Her heart sank. She got up hastily and looked in the glass; then lit a cigarette and threw herself into an armchair with her legs crossed – a boyish pose that her mother would certainly have denounced as vile, only Anna had gone too far even to bother imagining what her mother would have said.

'Cripes, I'd love to, Ernie, but I don't know that I can,' she said.

'What's the difficulty?' asked Ernest, leaning forward

with his pudgy hands clasped and a look of fresh anxiety on his face.

'It's hard to explain, Ernie,' she said, taking a puff of her cigarette and managing to look as brassy as three film stars.

'Is there another man?' he asked, growing pale.

'Ah, not at all!' she said impatiently, wishing to God he wouldn't always be trying to keep three jumps ahead so as to maintain his pose of omniscience.

'You needn't be afraid to tell me, you know,' he said in a manly tone. 'I don't mind if there is another man. I don't even mind if you've got a kid already.'

'A what?' she asked with a start.

'A kid. Lots of girls do.'

'They don't here,' she said, growing red and thinking that girls in England must have great nerve. 'It isn't that at all, only that I'm a Catholic.'

'Are you really, Anna?' Ernest asked with interest and real pleasure. 'I always thought you were an RC.'

'That's the same thing, surely,' she said.

'Is it?' he asked doubtfully. He hated to be caught out on a matter of fact.

'Oh, I'm sure it is. And anyway it seems I can't marry a Protestant.'

'But why not, Anna? I don't mind.'

'Other people do, though. I don't understand the half of it myself. It's Ma – she's dotty on religion. You could ask her.'

'I will,' Ernest said grimly. She could see from the battle-light in his eyes that he was looking forward to the scene. He loved scenes.

Mrs Martin was sitting by the fire in the kitchen, and when they came in, she fluttered in great concern about Ernest, but for once he was too angry for ceremony. He took a kitchen chair and rested one knee on it, smiling crookedly like a sunset in a stormy sky.

'Mrs Martin, Anna says she can't marry me because of my religion,' he said in a low, complaining tone. 'Is that true?'

'Oh, are ye going to be married, Ernest?' Mrs Martin cried joyously, not forgetting her own manners in spite of

79

his bad ones. 'Well, well, this is a great surprise! I think she's very lucky, Ernest; indeed, I do, and I hope you'll be very happy.'

Ernest again gave her a wry smile, but refused to let go of the chair and embrace her tenderly the way she expected.

'I don't see how we can be,' he said.

'Ah, that's nothing,' Mrs Martin said with a shrug and a giggle. 'Where there's a will there's a way, Ernest. We'll soon get round that. Of course,' she added, just to show him how simple it was, 'if you were a Catholic, you could be married in the morning.'

'No doubt, but you see, I'm not,' Ernest went on remorselessly. 'I was brought up Church of England, and I see nothing wrong with it.'

'And why would you?' cried Mrs Martin. 'I had some very dear friends who were Church of England. Indeed, they were better than a good many of our own. You might even be able to get a dispensation,' she added, going on her knees with the poker, a tactical position that enabled her to look at him or not as it suited her.

'A dispensation?' repeated Ernest. 'What's that?'

'It's really permission from the Pope.' She gave him a quick glance over her shoulder. 'You understand, of course – I needn't tell you that – the children would have to be brought up Catholics.'

'It's nothing to me how they're brought up,' said Ernest. 'That's Anna's look-out.'

'We could try it,' Mrs Martin said doubtfully, and Anna knew from her tone that she didn't mean a word of it. Ernest, poor lamb, was not smart enough to see how he was being outflanked by the old witch. He had given too much ground, and now that he was shaken, Mrs Martin was not going to be satisfied with a compromise like a dispensation. A son-in-law who dug with the wrong foot, indeed! She was out to make a convert of him, and Anna knew he hadn't a chance against her. 'Wouldn't that fire melt you?' Mrs Martin added wearily. 'Of course,' she went on, hoisting herself back into her chair, ' 'twouldn't be much of a marriage.'

'Why not?' asked Ernest. 'What would be wrong with it?'

'You'd have to be married out of the diocese,' Mrs Martin said cheerfully, not concealing the fact that she looked on a marriage that the Mahoneys couldn't see as not much better than open scandal. 'Wales, I believe is the nearest place. You can imagine what the neighbours would say about that. Wisha, do ye have people like that in England, Ernest?' she asked in amusement.

'God Almighty, wouldn't you think mixed marriages were catching?' Anna said, chagrined to see him so helpless. 'A wonder they wouldn't put us up in the Fever Hospital as they're at it.'

Her mother promptly saw her abandoning the cause of religion through human weakness and adopted the meek air she wore when she was really piqued.

'Of course, if that's how Anna feels, I don't see why ye wouldn't get married in a register office,' she said. 'I suppose 'tis as good as anything else.'

'Mrs Martin,' Ernest said with great dignity, dominating her, or at any rate imagining he was doing so. 'I don't expect Anna to do anything she doesn't think right, but I have principles too, remember. My religion means as much to me as hers to her.'

'I hope it means a good deal more, Ernest,' she said abjectly, getting in an extra poke at Anna under his guard. 'I'd be long sorry to think that was all it meant to you ... But you see, Ernest, there is a difference,' she added with great humility. 'We look on ourselves as the One True Church.'

'And what do you think we look on ourselves as?' Ernest asked sharply. 'Mrs Martin,' he went on appealingly with a throb of manly pathos in his voice, 'why should you despise a man merely because he worships at a different altar?'

'Oh, I wouldn't say we despised anybody, Ernest,' Mrs Martin said in alarm, fearing she might have gone too far. Then her tone grew grave again. 'But 'tisn't alike, you know.'

'Isn't it?'

'No, Ernest. The Catholic Church was founded by Our

Blessed Lord when he appointed St Peter to be His vicar on earth. St Peter is not quite the same thing as Henry VIII, Ernest.'

She looked at Ernest with a triumphant little smile, but it was revealed to her that Ernest did not know the first thing about Henry VIII – the history of his own country at that! Indeed, he seemed to take her remark as some sort of reflection on royalty.

'And what is the difference, Mrs Martin?' he asked.

'And all the wives, Ernest?' she replied meekly.

'Doesn't that depend on the wives, Mrs Martin?' Ernest said, refusing to be put down. 'Some men are luckier than others in the women they marry. He may have been one of the unlucky ones.' At this he really began to get into his stride. 'You know, Mrs Martin, I don't think you should judge a man's conduct unless you know all about his circumstances. People are sometimes nothing like so bad as they're made out to be. Often they're very good people who find themselves in circumstances beyond their own control ... Anyhow, I'm marrying Anna, even if I have to become a Mohammedan, but at the same time I must say that I consider it unnecessary and unfair. I shouldn't be honest with myself or you unless I made that clear.'

'Ah, well, maybe you'll think differently when you know us a bit better,' Mrs Martin said without rancour as she spread the tablecloth for supper. 'Though indeed, Ernest,' she added with a wounded giggle that showed what she thought of Ernest's bad taste, 'I hope you'll find we're a cut above Mohammedans.'

Anna had to butt in to prevent Ernest from glorifying Mohammedans. That was one of the troubles about a man who knew everything like Ernest: he was so confoundedly tolerant that he was always picking quarrels with those who were not.

Three

Next evening Anna brought Ernest to the convent, a large hospital on a hill overlooking the town. This was where the nuns gave instructions to would-be converts. There was a statue of the Sacred Heart on the lawn, a statue of the Blessed Virgin in the hall, and a coloured statue of St Joseph at the end of the corridor. Ernest tried to walk with a careless, masculine swing but skated on the polished floor, got red, and swore. When they entered a parlour with open windows, a bookcase and a picture of the Holy Family, he looked so sorry for himself that Anna's heart was wrung.

'And you won't forget to call her "Sister", Ernie, will you?' she whispered appealingly.

'I'll try, Anna,' Ernest said wearily, slumped in his chair with his head hanging. 'I can't guarantee anything.'

The door opened and in bounced Mrs Martin's friend, Sister Angela, beaming at them with an array of prominent teeth. She had a rather good-looking, emaciated face with a big-boned nose, and an intensely excitable manner exacerbated by deafness. Mrs Martin said in her modest way that quite a lot of people looked on Sister Angela as one of the three great intellects of Europe, which she seemed to think was the same thing as her other favourite remark, that 'poor Sister Angela was very simple and childish'. She had been for years the bosom friend of the old parish priest who had visions, and she was now collecting evidence to have him beatified. She had cut up and distributed his nightshirts among the poor as relics, and one of his trousers, used as a belt, was supposed to have turned one of the city drunkards into a model husband.

She wrung both their hands simultaneously, beaming sharply from one to the other with a birdlike cock of her head. Like all deaf people she relied as much on expression as speech.

'Anna, dear!' she said breathlessly. 'So delighted when your mother told me. And this is your fiancé? Quite a handsome man! What's his name? Speak up!'

Anna shouted.

'Thompson?' Sister Angela cried as though this were a most delightful and unexpected coincidence. 'He's not one of us, your mother says,' she added, lowering her voice. 'What persuasion is he?'

'Church of England,' said Anna.

'Not a bit,' said Sister Angela, shaking her head vigorously.

'I said he was Church of England,' bawled Anna.

'Oooh! Church of England?' hooted Sister Angela, her face lighting up. Anna noticed she had really lovely eyes. 'So near and yet so far,' she said. 'But we never have any difficulty,' she added firmly. 'Last month,' she said to Ernest, 'we had a sun-worshipper.'

'You didn't!' said Anna. 'And did he turn?'

'I didn't like him,' Sister Angela said, clamping her lips and shaking her head as she stared into the fireplace. She had a tendency to drop out of conversations as unexpectedly as she burst in on them. 'He was a mechanic. You'd think he'd know better. So silly!' She entered the conversation again with a smile in Anna's direction. 'I wouldn't say he was sincere, would you?'

'I'll leave ye to it,' Anna said in a panic, knowing well that at any moment Ernest was liable to break into an impassioned defence of sun-worshippers. In fact, he had told her already that it was a religion that appealed to him a lot. He would not like to hear it described as silly. When she turned at the door to smile at him she failed to catch his eye, and it grieved her to see the trapped look on his handsome, sulky face.

She waited for him in a little paper-shop opposite the convent. When he came out she knew at once that things had gone wrong because he kept his head down and failed to raise his hat to her.

'Well?' she asked gaily. 'How did you get on?'

'It's hard to say,' he said moodily, striding on without looking at her. 'I've listened to some tall stories in my life, but she takes the biscuit.'

'But what did she say?' wailed Anna.

'She had nothing to say,' Ernest replied with gloomy triumph. 'I refuted her on every single point.'

'She must have loved that,' said Anna ironically.

'She didn't,' said Ernest. 'Women never appreciate clear, logical discussion. You'd think if Catholicism meant so much to them, they'd have men to teach it.'

'And did you call her "Sister"?'

'No, she didn't sound much like a sister to me. She said, "I thought you were Church of England," and I said, "I was brought up Church of England, but for many years I've been a disciple of Abou Ben Adhem." She hadn't even heard of Abou Ben Adhem!'

'Go on!' Anna said despairingly. 'And who was he when he was at home?'

'Abou Ben Adhem?' Ernest said. 'He was the man who said to the angel: "Write me as one who loved his fellow-men." Abou Ben Adhem has been the great religious inspiration of my life,' he added reverently.

'Well, I hope he inspires you now,' said Anna. 'That one will be after you with a carving knife.'

Knowledgeable and all as he was, Ernest simply had no idea how serious the situation had become. Seeing Anna so depressed, he cheered up, and told her that he would make things all right next day: it was just that he hadn't been feeling well, and women were so illogical anyway. For the future he'd swallow everything that Sister Angela said. Anna told him that he didn't know what he was talking about. For a man to suggest doubts of the Bleeding Statues of Templemore or the Apparitions of Annaghishin was to go looking for trouble. For once her mother agreed with her. Mrs Martin, who had been married to one of them, knew only too well the harm men with loose tongues could do themselves with neighbours like the Mahoneys around. She treated it as a major crisis; put on her best things and went off to the convent herself.

When she returned she looked more apologetic than ever and fluttered about the house, fussing over trifles with a crucified air till she got on Anna's nerves.

'Well?' Anna bawled when she could bear it no longer.

'Aren't you going to tell us what she said?'

'Sister Angela?' Mrs Martin breathed lightly. 'She's not seeing anybody.'

'Go on!' Anna said with a cold hand on her heart. 'What ails her?'

'She's too upset,' Mrs Martin said almost joyously. 'She won't be able to go on with the instruction. She's afraid he'll upset her faith. He wasn't Church of England at all, but some religion they'd never heard of.'

'I know; an Abou Ben Something,' said Anna.

'Ah, well, if 'twas any decent sort of religion they'd know about it,' her mother said with resignation. 'They think it's probably something like the Dippers. Of course, I knew he wasn't a gentleman. Church of England people are well brought up. Reverend Mother gave me the name of a Dominican theologian, but she thinks herself you'd better have no more to do with him.'

'How soft she has it!' blazed Anna. 'To suit her, I suppose.'

'Maybe you'd better instruct him yourself,' giggled her mother.

'I will,' said Anna. 'And make a better job of it than them.'

She put on her coat and strode blindly out without a notion of where she was going. It was dark night by this time, and she walked up the hill past the Mahoneys' shop and said as she did so: 'Blast ye, anyway! Ye're just as bad.' Then she found herself beside the church, a plain, low, towerless church which lay on top of the hill with its soft lights burning like the ark left high on top of Mount Ararat. The thought that she might never come down the steps of it in wreath and veil gave her courage. She knew there was a new curate in the presbytery, and that he was young like herself.

When the housekeeper showed her in, he was sitting before the fire, listening to the wireless, a handsome young man with a knobby face. He got up, smiling, one hand in his trousers pocket, the other outstretched.

'I'm Anna Martin,' Anna said, plunging straight into her business, 'and I'm engaged to an English bloke that's over here at the new factory. He wants to turn, but he can't make head or tail of what the nuns tell him.'

'Sit down and tell me about him,' said the curate amiably, turning off the wireless. 'Will you have a fag?'

'I will,' said Anna, crossing her legs and opening her coat. 'As true as God,' she said, her lip beginning to quiver, 'I'm nearly dotty with it.'

'What religion is he?' asked the curate, holding out a lighted match to her.

'An Abou Ben Something,' replied Anna, screwing up her eyes from the smoke. 'You never heard of it?'

'I did not,' said the curate. 'I thought you said he was English.'

'He is, too,' said Anna. 'I don't know much about it. 'Tis something about loving your neighbour – the usual stuff! And damn little love there is when you start looking for it,' she added bitterly.

'Do you take a drink?' asked the curate.

'I do,' said Anna, who thought he was a pet.

'Don't worry any more about it,' he advised, pouring her out a glass of sherry. 'We'll make him all right for you.'

'You'll have no trouble as long as you don't mind what he says,' Anna said eagerly. 'He's the best fellow in the world only he likes to hear himself talk.'

' 'Tis a good man's fault,' said the curate.

Next evening, outside the presbytery gate, Anna gave Ernest his final instructions. Desperation had changed her. She was now masterful and precise to the point of vindictiveness, and Ernest was unusually subdued.

'And mind you call him "Father",' she said sharply.

'All right, all right,' said Ernest sulkily. 'I won't forget.'

'And whatever the hell you do, don't contradict him,' said Anna. 'There's nothing they hate like being contradicted.'

Then feeling she had done everything in her power, she went into the little church to say a prayer. Afterwards she met Ernest outside, and had every reason to feel gratified. He and the curate had got on like a house afire.

'Isn't he a delightful fellow?' Ernest chuckled enthusiastically. 'And what a brain! It's positively a pleasure to argue with him.' Ernest was himself again, his face shining, his eyes popping. 'You see, Anna, I told you that woman had no brains.'

After that it was almost impossible to keep him away from the presbytery, instruction or no instruction. He courted the curate with considerably more warmth than he courted Anna. He repaired the curate's shotgun and practically rewired the whole presbytery, and in return the curate told him all the things he wanted to know about clerical life. Ernest even began to see himself as a priest; celibacy, which to him might have been a major obstacle, was explained when you realized how free it left you to deal with other people's sex life, and Ernest enjoyed other people's sex life almost more than he did his own. Ernest was nothing if not broad-minded.

One Saturday afternoon, six weeks later, he made his profession of faith and renounced all his previous heresies, including Abou Ben Adhemism, made his first confession, was baptised and received absolution for all the sins of his past life. Unfortunately, the Mahoneys had got hold of the convent version of it and were putting it about that he was a Turk. Mrs Martin countered this by exaggerating, in her deprecating way, his wealth, rank, and education – of course, his family was only upper middle class and his salary only a thousand a year, but then, you couldn't expect everything.

He cut a splendid figure coming from the altar with Anna, in a new suit specially bought for the occasion, his hands joined and a look of childish beatitude on his big, fat, good-natured face.

Four

It was too good to be true, of course. It all became clear to Anna on the boat off Holyhead when Ernest disappeared into the saloon and only emerged half-seas-over. She had never seen him drunk before and she didn't like it. He was hysterical, jubilant, swaggering, and there was a wild look in his eyes.

'What's wrong, Ernie?' she said impatiently, staring hard at him.

'Wrong?' replied Ernest with a shrill laugh. 'What could be wrong?'

'That's what I want to know,' Anna said quietly. 'And I'm not going any farther with you till I do know.'

'Why?' he asked in the same wild tone. 'Do I look like someone there was something wrong with?'

'You look as if you were scared out of your wits,' Anna said candidly.

That sobered him. He leaned over the side of the boat, flushed and wry-faced as though he were going to be sick. The sunlit water was reflected up on to his big, heavy-jowled face, and he no longer looked handsome. He scarcely looked human.

'You didn't pinch anything, did you?' she asked anxiously.

'No, Anna,' he replied, beginning to sob, 'it's not that.'

'I suppose you're going to tell me that you're married already?'

He nodded a couple of times, too full for speech.

'That's grand,' she said with bitter restraint, already hearing the comments of the Mahoneys. 'And kids, I suppose?'

'Two,' sobbed Ernest, and buried his head in his arms.

'Sweet of you to tell me,' she said, growing white.

'Well, can you blame me?' he asked wildly, drawing himself up with what was almost dignity. 'I loved you. I knew from the first moment that you were the only woman in the world for me. I had to have you.'

'Oh, you had me all right, Ernie,' said Anna, unable, even at this most solemn moment of her life, to be anything but common.

But in spite of all his pleadings she refused to go beyond Holyhead with him. Her childhood training had been too strong, and though she might be common, she wouldn't deliberately do anything she thought really wrong. She felt sure she was going to have a baby: that was the only thing lacking to her degradation. And it all came of going with foreigners.

In the weeks that followed, she almost came to admire her mother. It was bad enough for Anna, but for her mother it was unredeemed catastrophe. Unless Father Jeremiah Mahoney not only left the Church but left it to live with a married woman or a Negress – a thing Mrs Martin was too conscientious even to desire – the war between herself and the Mahoneys was over. But she wasn't going to let herself be dislodged on that account. Under all the convent-school fatuity was the stout, sensible peasant stuff. She even approved of Anna's decision to give no information to the police, who were after Ernest. Even the prospect of a baby she accepted as the will of God – anything that couldn't be concealed from the Mahoneys seemed to be her definition of the will of God.

But Anna couldn't take things in that spirit. The whole neighbourhood was humming with spite. When she went into town she ran the gauntlet of malicious eyes and tongues. 'She knew, she knew! Sure, of course, she knew! Didn't Sister Angela warn them what he was? All grandeur and false pride. She wanted to say she could get a husband – a pasty-faced thing like that.' But it wasn't only the spite. Every second day she got some heart-rending appeal from Ernest not to let him down and threatening to kill himself. She knew she shouldn't open his letters, but she couldn't keep off them. She read and re-read them. That is what I mean by the influence of a foreigner. Things that had been as natural as breathing to Anna suddenly began to seem queer. She didn't know why she was doing them or why anyone else expected her to do them. Under the strain her character began to change. She grew explosive.

One night she had been sitting in the back kitchen, listening to her mother and a neighbour whispering in the shop, and when the neighbour left, Anna came to the inner door and leaned against the jamb with folded arms, blowsy and resentful.

'Who was the "poor Anna" ye were talking about?' she asked casually.

'Ah, indeed, Anna, you may well ask,' sighed her mother.

'But why "poor"?' Anna went on reasonably. 'I didn't marry a boozer that knocked me about like that old one did. I'm going to have a kid, which is more than a lot of the old serpents will ever have.'

'I'm glad you appreciate it,' her mother said waspishly. 'I hope you tell everyone. They'll be all delighted you're not down-hearted about it.'

'Why?' asked Anna. 'Am I supposed to be down-hearted?'

'Why should you be?' said her mother. 'Haven't you every reason for being cheerful?'

'That's exactly what I was thinking,' Anna said in a heart-breaking drawl. 'It just crossed my mind that I wasn't suited to this place at all.' Then, as she heard her own voice speaking, she was aghast. 'Cripes!' she thought in her common way. 'There goes the blooming china.' She was exactly like the last maid giving notice after breaking the last of the Henebry-Hayes china off the kitchen wall. She realized that at that moment there was not a drop of Henebry-Hayes blood left in her veins; from head to foot she was pure Martin; a woman of no class. 'I'm not grand enough for this place,' she went on recklessly. 'I think I'll have to go somewhere I'm better suited.'

She was suddenly filled with a great sense of liberation and joy. The strain of being a real Henebry-Hayes is something you cannot appreciate until it is lifted. Then she went upstairs and wrote to Ernest, telling him when to expect her.

Under the circumstances, it was perhaps the best thing she could have done. Once those foreign notions have found their way into your mind, it is impossible ever to expel them entirely afterwards.

The Common Chord (1947)

JUDAS

'Sure you won't be late, Jerry?' the mother said and I going out.

'Am I ever late?' I said, and I laughed.

That was all we said, but it stuck in my mind. As I was going down the road I was thinking it was months since I'd taken her to the pictures. Of course, you might think that funny, but after the father's death we were thrown together a lot. And I knew she hated being alone in the house after dark.

At the same time I had my own troubles. You see, being an only child I never knocked round the way other fellows did. All the fellows in the office went with girls, or at any rate let on that they did. They said: 'Who was the old doll I saw you with the other night, Jerry? You'd better mind yourself, or you'll be getting into trouble.' To hear them talk, you'd imagine there was no sport in the world only girls, and that they'd always be getting you into trouble. Paddy Kinnane, for instance, always talked like that, and he never saw how it upset me. I think he thought it a great compliment. It wasn't until years after that I began to suspect that Paddy's acquaintance with girls was about of one kind with my own.

Then I met Kitty Doherty. Kitty was a hospital nurse, and all the chaps in the office said a fellow should never go with hospital nurses. Ordinary girls were bad enough, but nurses were a fright – they knew too much. When I met Kitty I knew that this was a lie. She was a well-educated, superior girl; she lived up the river in a posh locality, and her mother was on all sorts of councils and committees. Kitty was small and wiry; a good-looking girl, always in good humour, and when she talked, she hopped from one subject to another like a robin on a frosty morning.

I used to meet her in the evening up the river road, as though I were walking there by accident and very surprised to see her. 'Fancy meeting you!' I'd say or, 'Well, well, isn't this a great surprise!' Mind you, it usually was, because no matter how much I was expecting her, I was never prepared for the shock of her presence. Then we'd stand talking for half an hour and I'd see her home. Several times she asked me in, but I was too nervous. I knew I'd lose my head, break the china, use some dirty word, and then go home and cut my throat. Of course, I never asked her to come to the pictures or anything of the sort. She was above all that. My only hope was that if I waited long enough I might be able to save her from drowning or the white slavers or something else dramatic, that would show in a modest and dignified way how I felt about her. At the same time I had a bad conscience because I knew I should stay at home more with the mother, but the very thought that I might be missing an opportunity of fishing Kitty out of the river would spoil a whole evening for me.

That night in particular I was nearly distracted. I had not seen Kitty for three weeks. I was sure that, at the very least, she was dying and asking for me, but that no one knew my address. A week before, I had felt I simply couldn't bear it any longer and made an excuse to go down to the post office. I rang up the hospital and asked for Kitty. I fully expected them to say in gloomy tones that Kitty had died half an hour before, and had the shock of my life when the girl at the other end asked my name. I lost my head. 'I'm afraid I'm a stranger to Miss Doherty,' I said with an embarrassed laugh. 'But I have a message for her from a friend.'

Then I became completely panic-stricken. What could a girl like Kitty make of a damned, deliberate lie like that? What else was it but a trap laid by an old and cunning hand? I held the receiver out and looked at it as if it were someone whose neck I was just going to wring. 'Moynihan,' I said to it, 'you're mad. An asylum, Moynihan, is the only place for you.'

I heard Kitty's voice, not in my ear at all, but in the telephone booth as though she were standing there with me, and I nearly dropped the receiver in terror. Then I raised it and asked in what I thought of as a French accent: 'Who is dat speaking, please?' 'This is Kitty Doherty,' she replied impatiently. 'Who are you?'

That was exactly what I was wondering myself. Who the blazes was I? 'I am Monsieur Bertrand,' I said cautiously. 'I am afraid I have the wrong number. I am so sorry.' Then I put down the receiver and thought how nice it would be if only I had a penknife handy to cut my throat. It's funny, but from the moment I met Kitty I was always coveting sharp things like razors and penknives. It didn't seem to me that there were enough of them in the world at all.

After that an awful idea dawned on me. Of course, I should have thought of it sooner, but, as you can see, I was not exactly knowledgeable where girls were concerned. I began to see that I was not meeting Kitty for the very good reason that Kitty did not want to meet me. What her objection was I could only imagine, but then imagination was my strong point. I examined my conscience to see what I might have said to upset her. I remembered every single remark I had made without exception, and unfortunately it was only too clear what her objection was because every single one was either brutal, indecent or disgusting. I had talked of Paddy Kinnane as a fellow who 'went with dolls'. What could a pure-minded girl think of a chap who naturally used such an expression except – what unfortunately was quite true – that he had a mind like a cesspit.

But this evening I felt more confident. It was a lovely summer evening with views of hillsides and fields between the gaps in the houses, and it raised my spirits. Perhaps I was wrong; perhaps she had not noticed or understood my filthy conversation; perhaps we might meet and walk home together. I walked the full length of the river road and back, and then started to walk it again. The crowds were thinning out as fellows and girls slipped off up the lanes or down the river-bank, courting. As the streets went out like lamps about me my hopes sank lower. I saw clearly that she was avoiding me because she knew that I was not the quiet, good-natured fellow I let on to be but a volcano of brutality and lust. 'Lust! lust! lust!' I hissed to myself, clenching my fists. I could have forgiven myself anything but the lust.

Then I glanced up and saw her on top of a tram. I instantly forgot about the lust and smiled and waved my cap at her, but she was looking ahead and did not see me. At least, I hoped she didn't see me. I raced after the tram, intending to jump on to it, sit in one of the back seats on top where she would not notice me, and then say in astonishment as she got off: 'Fancy meeting you here.' But as if the driver knew exactly what was in my mind, he put on speed, and the old tram went bucketing and screeching down the one straight bit of road in the whole town, and I stood panting in the roadway, smiling as though missing a tram were the best joke in the world, and wishing all the time that I had a penknife and the courage to use it. My position was hopeless!

Then I must have gone a bit mad – really mad, I mean – because I started to race the tram. There were still a lot of people out walking, and they stared after me in an incredulous way, so I lifted my fists to my chest in the attitude of a professional runner and dropped into what I hoped would look like a comfortable stride and delude them into the belief that I was training for a big race. By the time I was finished, I *was* a runner, and full of indignation against the people who still continued to stare at me.

Between my running and the tram's halts I just managed to keep it in view as far as the other side of town. When I saw Kitty get off and go up a hilly street I collapsed and was only able to drag myself after her. When she went into a house on the terrace above the road I sat on the high curb with my head between my knees till the panting stopped. At least, I had run her to earth. I could afford to rest and walk up and down before the house till she came out and then say with an innocent smile: 'Fancy meeting you!'

But my luck was dead out that night. As I walked up and down, close enough to the house to keep it in view but not close enough to be seen from the windows, I saw a tall man strolling up at the opposite side of the road and my heart sank. It was Paddy Kinnane.

'Hallo, Jerry,' he chuckled with that knowing grin he put on whenever he wanted to compliment you on being discovered in a compromising situation. 'What are you doing here?'

'Just waiting for a chap I had a date with, Paddy,' I said trying to sound casual.

'Looks more to me as if you were waiting for an old doll,' Paddy said flatteringly. 'Still waters run deep. When were you supposed to meet him?'

Cripes, I didn't even know what the time was!

'Half eight,' I said at random.

'Half eight?' said Paddy. ' 'Tis nearly nine now.'

'Ah, he's a most unpunctual fellow,' I said angrily. 'He's always the same. He'll turn up all right.'

'I may as well wait with you,' said Paddy, leaning against the wall and taking out a packet of cigarettes. 'You might find yourself stuck at the end of the evening. There's people in this town who have no consideration for anyone.'

That was Paddy all out – a heart of gold, no trouble too much for him if he could do you a good turn – I'd have loved to strangle him. I knew there was nothing for it but to make a fresh start.

'Ah, to hell with him!' I said impatiently. 'I won't bother waiting any longer. It only struck me this minute that I have another appointment – up the Western Road. You'll excuse me now, Paddy. I'll tell you about it another time.'

And back I went to the tramline. I caught a tram and went on to the farther terminus, near Kitty's house. There, at least, Paddy Kinnane could not get at me. I sat on the river wall in the dusk. The moon was rising, and every fifteen minutes a tram came grunting and squeaking over the old bridge and went black-out as the conductor switched his trolley. Each time I got off the wall and stood on the curb in the moonlight, searching for Kitty among the passengers. Then a policeman came along, and, as he seemed suspicious of me, I slunk slowly off up the hill and stood against a wall in shadow. There was a high wall at the other side of the road, and behind it the roof of a house was cut out of the sky in moonlight. Every now and then a tram came in and people passed, and the snatches of conversation I caught were like the warmth from an open door to the heart of a homeless man. It was quite clear now that my position was hopeless. If Kitty had walked or been driven she would have reached home from the opposite direction. She could be at home in bed by now. The last tram came and went, and still there was no Kitty, and still I hung on despairingly. While one glimmer of a chance remained I could not go home.

Then I heard a woman's step. I could not even pretend to myself that it might be Kitty till she suddenly shuffled past me with that hasty little stride. I started and called her name. She glanced quickly over her shoulder and, seeing a man emerge from the shadow, took fright and ran. I ran too, but she put on speed and began to leave me behind. At this I despaired and shouted after her at the top of my voice.

'Kitty! Kitty! For God's sake, wait!'

She ran a few steps further and then halted incredulously. She looked back, and then turned and slowly retraced her steps.

'Jerry Moynihan!' she whispered in astonishment. 'What are you doing here?'

I was summoning strength to tell her that I had happened to be taking a stroll in that direction and was surprised to see her when I realized the improbability of it and began to cry instead. Then I laughed. It was hysteria, I suppose. But Kitty had had a bad fright, and, now that she was getting over it, she was as cross as two sticks.

'Are you out of your mind or what?' she snapped.

'But I didn't see you for weeks,' I said.

'What about it?' she asked. 'I wasn't out.'

'I thought it might be something I said to you,' I said desperately.

'What did you say?' she asked, but I could not repeat any of the hideous things I knew I had said. I might, by accident, repeat one she hadn't noticed.

'Oh, anything,' I said.

'Oh, it's not that,' she said impatiently. 'It's just Mother.'

'Why, is there something wrong with her?' I asked almost joyously. A nice fatal or near-fatal illness might just provide me with the opportunity I needed for rushing to her rescue.

'No, but she made such a fuss of it, I felt it wasn't worth it.'

'A fuss? A fuss about what?'

'About you, of course,' Kitty said in exasperation.

This was worse than anything I had imagined. A woman I had never met in my life making a fuss about me. This was really terrible!

'But what did I do?' I asked.

'You didn't *do* anything, but people were talking about us just the same. And you wouldn't come in and meet her like anyone else. I know she's a bit of a fool, and her head is stuffed with old nonsense about her family. I could never see that they were different to anybody else, and anyway, she married a commercial traveller herself, so she has nothing much to talk about. Still, you needn't be so superior.'

I began to shiver all over. I had thought of Kitty as a secret between God, herself and me, and assumed that she only knew the half of it. Now it seemed that I didn't even know the half. People were talking about us! I was superior! What next?

'But what has she against me?' I asked, wondering if she had a spy in the office, reporting on things I said and did.

'She thinks we're doing a big tangle, of course,' snapped Kitty as though she were surprised at my stupidity. 'I suppose she imagines you're not grand enough for a great-great-grandniece of Daniel O'Connell. I told her you were above that sort of thing, but she wouldn't believe me. She said I was a deep, callous, crafty little intriguer and that I hadn't a drop of Daniel O'Connell's blood in my veins.' Kitty giggled at the thought of herself as an intriguer, and no wonder.

'That's all she knows,' I said despairingly.

'I know,' Kitty agreed sadly. 'The woman has no sense. And anyway she has no reason to think I'd tell her lies. Cissy and I always had fellows, and we spooned with them all over the shop under her very nose, so I don't see why she thinks I'm trying to conceal anything now.'

At this I laughed like an idiot. This was worse than appalling. This was nightmare. Kitty, whom I had thought so angelic, talking in cold blood of 'spooning'. Even the bad women in the bad books I had read didn't talk about love-making in that cold-blooded way. Madame Bovary herself had the decency to pretend that she didn't like it. It was another door opening on an outside world, but Kitty thought I was laughing at her and began to apologize.

'Of course, I had no sense,' she said. 'You were the first fellow that treated me properly. The others only wanted to fool around, and now, because I don't like it, Mother is convinced I've got into something really ghastly. I can see her looking at me sideways to see is my figure all right. She really is a bit dotty. I told her I liked you better than any other fellow I knew, but that I'd grown out of that sort of thing.'

'And what did she say to that?' I asked. I was beginning to see that imagination was not enough. All round me there was an objective reality that was a thousand times more nightmarish than any fantasy of my own, and I wanted to know about it, though at the same time it turned my stomach.

'Ah, I told you she was silly,' Kitty said in embarrassment.

'Go on!' I said desperately.

'Well,' said Kitty with a demure grin, 'she said you were a deep, designing guttersnipe who knew exactly how to get round feather-pated little idiots like me . . . I suppose I'm not clever, but I'm not as stupid as all that . . . But you see, it's quite hopeless. I think she's a bit common. She doesn't understand.'

'Oh, God!' I said, almost in tears. 'I only wish I was.'

'You wish you were what?' she asked.

'A deep, designing whatever she called me. Because then I might have some chance with you.'

Kitty looked at me for a moment, and I could see she was wondering about something.

'To tell the truth, I thought you were a bit keen on me at first, but then I wasn't sure. I mean, you didn't give any indication.'

'God, when I think what I've been through in the past few weeks!' I said bitterly.

'I know,' said Kitty. 'I was a bit fed up myself. You get used to people, I suppose.'

Then we said nothing for a few moments. It didn't seem to me there was much more to be said.

'You're sure now you mean it?' she asked.

'But I tell you I was on the point of committing suicide,' I said angrily.

'Ah, what good would that be?' she asked with another shrug, and this time she looked at me and laughed outright – the little jade!

I insisted on telling her about my prospects. She didn't want to hear about my prospects; she wanted me to kiss her, but that seemed to me a very sissy sort of occupation, so I told her just the same, in the intervals. It was as if a stone had been lifted off my heart, and I went home in the moonlight, singing. Then I heard the clock strike, and the singing stopped. I remembered the mother's 'Sure you won't be late?' and my own 'Am I ever late?' This was desperation too, but of a different sort.

The door was ajar and the kitchen in darkness. I saw her sitting before the fire by herself, and just as I was about to throw my arms round her, I smelt Kitty's perfume and was afraid to go near her. God help us, as though that would have told her anything!

'Hullo, Mum,' I said with a nervous laugh, rubbing my hands. 'You're all in darkness.'

'You'll have a cup of tea?' she said.

'I might as well.'

'What time is it?' she said, lighting the gas. 'You're very late.'

'I met a fellow from the office,' I said, but at the same time I was stung by the complaint in her tone.

'You frightened me,' she said with a little whimper. 'I didn't know what happened you. What kept you at all?'

'Oh, what do you think?' I said, goaded by my own sense of guilt. 'Drinking and blackguarding as usual.'

I could have bitten my tongue off as I said it; it sounded so cruel, as if some stranger had said it instead of me. She turned to me with a frightened stare as if she were seeing the stranger too, and somehow I couldn't bear it.

'God Almighty!' I said. 'A fellow can have no life in his own house.'

I went hastily upstairs, lit the candle, undressed, and got into bed. A chap could be a drunkard and blackguard and not be made to suffer what I was being made to suffer for being out late one single night. This, I felt, was what you got for being a good son.

'Jerry,' she called from the foot of the stairs, 'will I bring you up your cup?'

'I don't want it now, thanks,' I said.

I heard her sigh and turn away. Then she locked the doors, front and back. She didn't wash up, and I knew that my cup of tea was standing on the table with a saucer on top in case I changed my mind. She came slowly upstairs and her walk was that of an old woman. I blew out the candle before she reached the landing, in case she came in to ask if I wanted anything else, and the moonlight came in the attic window and brought me memories of Kitty. But every time I tried to imagine her face as she grinned up at me, waiting for me to kiss her, it was the mother's face that came up instead, with that look like a child's when you strike him for the first time – as if he suddenly saw the stranger in you. I remembered all our life together from the night my father died; our early Mass on Sunday; our visits to the pictures, and our plans for the future, and Christ! it was as if I was inside her mind while she sat by the fire waiting for the blow to fall. And now it had fallen, and I was a stranger to her, and nothing I could ever do would make us the same to one another again. There was something like a cannon-ball stuck in my chest, and I lay awake till the cocks started crowing. Then I could bear it no longer. I went out on the landing and listened.

'Are you awake, Mother?' I asked in a whisper.

'What is it, Jerry?' she replied in alarm, and I knew that she hadn't slept any more than I had.

'I only came to say I was sorry,' I said, opening the door of her room, and then as I saw her sitting up in bed under the Sacred Heart lamp, the cannon-ball burst inside me and I began to cry like a kid.

'Oh, child, child, child,' she exclaimed; 'what are you crying for at all, my little boy?' She spread out her arms to me. I went to her and she hugged me and rocked me as she did when I was only a nipper. 'Oh, oh, oh,' she was saying to herself in a whisper, 'my storeen bawn, my little man!' – all the names she hadn't called me in years. That was all we said. I couldn't bring myself to tell her what I had done, nor could she confess to me that she was jealous: all she could do was to try and comfort me for the way I'd hurt her, to make up to me for the nature she had given me. 'My storeen bawn!' she said. 'My little man!'

The Common Chord (1947)

THE MIRACLE

Vanity, according to the Bishop, was the Canon's great weakness, and there might be some truth in that. He was a tall, good-looking man with a big chin and a manner of deceptive humility. He deplored the fact that so many of the young priests came from poor homes where good manners were not taught, and looked back regretfully to the old days when, according to him, every parish priest read his Virgil. He gave himself out for an authority on food and wine, and ground and brewed his own coffee. He refused to live in the ramshackle old presbytery that had served generations of priests, and had built himself a residence second only to the Bishop's palace and furnished with considerably more taste and expense. There he ate his meals with the right wines, brewed his coffee and sipped his green chartreuse, and occasionally dipped into ecclesiastical history. He liked to read about days when the clergy were really well off.

It was distasteful to the Canon that the lower classes should be creeping into the Church and gaining high office in it, but it was a real heartbreak to him that its functions and privileges were being usurped by new men and methods, and that miracles were now being performed out of bottles and syringes. He would have preferred surgeons to remain tradesmen and barbers as they had been in the good old days and, though he would have been astonished to hear it himself, was as jealous as a prima donna at the interference of Bobby Healy, the doctor, with his flock.

There was certainly some truth in the Bishop's criticism. The Canon hated competition; he liked young Dr Devaney, who affected to believe that medicine was all hocus-pocus, and took a grave view of Bobby Healy, who didn't. This caused Bobby's practice to go down quite a bit. When the Canon visited a dying man he took care to ask who the doctor was. If it was Bobby Healy he nodded and looked grave, and everyone knew Bobby had killed the unfortunate patient as usual. When the two men met the Canon was courteous and condescending, Bobby respectful and obliging, and nobody could ever have told from the doctor's face whether or not he knew what was going on. But there was very little Bobby didn't know. There is a certain sort of guile that goes deeper than any cleric's – the peasant's guile. Dr Healy had that.

But there was one person in his parish whom the Canon disliked even more than he disliked the doctor. That was a man called Bill Enright. Nominally, Bill was a farmer and breeder of greyhounds; really, he was the last of a family of bandits who had terrorized the countryside for generations. He was a tall, gaunt man with fair hair and a small golden moustache; perfectly rosy skin like a baby's, and a pair of bright blue eyes that seemed to expand into a wide, unwinking, animal glare. His cheekbones were so high that they gave the impression of cutting his skin, and gave his eyes an oriental slant. With its low, sharp-sloping forehead, his whole face seemed to point outward to the sharp tip of his nose and then retreat again in a pair of high teeth, very sharp and very white, a drooping lower lip, and a small, weak feminine chin.

Now, Bill, as he would be the first to tell you, was not a bad man. He was a traditionalist and did as his father and grandfather had done before him. He had gone to Mass and the sacraments and even paid his dues, and been in every way prepared to treat the Canon as a bandit of similar dignity to himself, but the Canon had merely been outraged by his presumption. Bill was notoriously living in sin with his housekeeper, Nellie Mahony from Doonamon, and the Canon had ordered her to leave the house. When she didn't, he went to her brothers and demanded that they should bring her home, but her brothers had too much experience of the Enrights to try such a risky experiment, and Nellie remained on, while Bill, declaring loudly that religion was all his eye, ceased going to Mass. People agreed that it wasn't altogether Bill's fault, and that the Canon could not brook another authority than his own – a hasty man!

To Bobby Healy, on the other hand, Bill was bound by the strongest tie that could bind an Enright, because the doctor had once cured a greyhound for him, the mother of King Kong. Four or five times a year the doctor was summoned to treat Bill for an overdose of whiskey; Bill owed him just as much money as was fitting to owe a friend, and all Bill's companions knew that when they were in trouble themselves, Dr Healy was the man. Whatever the Canon might think, Bill was one it paid to stand in well with.

One spring day Bobby got one of his usual summonses to the presence. Bill lived in a fine Georgian house a mile outside the town. It had once belonged to the Rowes, but Bill had got them out by making their lives a hell. The avenue was overgrown, and the house with its fine Ionic portico looked dirty and dilapidated. Two dogs got up and barked at him in a neighbourly way. They hated it when Bill was sick and they knew that Bobby had a knack of putting him on his feet again.

Nellie Mahony opened the door. She was a small, fat country girl with a rosy complexion and mass of jet-black hair that shone almost as brilliantly as her eyes. The doctor, who was sometimes seized with such fits of amiable idiocy, gave her a squeeze and she replied with a shriek of laughter that broke off suddenly.

'Wisha, Dr Healy, oughtn't you to be ashamed, and the state we're in?' she asked complainingly.

'How's that, Nellie?' he asked. 'Isn't it the usual thing?'

'The usual thing?' she shrieked. She had a trick of snatching up and repeating someone's final words in a brilliant tone, a full octave higher, like a fiddle repeating a phrase from the double bass. Then with dramatic abruptness she let her voice drop to a whisper and dabbed her eyes with her apron. 'He's dying, doctor,' she said.

'For God's sake!' whispered the doctor. Life had rubbed down his principles considerably, and the fact that Bill was suspected of a share in at least one murder did not prejudice him in the least. 'Sure, I saw him in town on Monday and he never looked better.'

'Never looked better?' echoed the fiddle, while Nellie's beautiful black eyes filled with a tragic emotion not far removed from joy. 'And then didn't he go out on the Tuesday morning on me, in the pouring rain, with three men and two dogs, and not come back till Friday night, with the result' – this was a boss phrase of Nellie's, always followed by a dramatic pause and change of key – 'that he caught a chill up through him and never left the bed since.'

'What are you saying to Bobby Healy?' a man's voice called from upstairs. It was nearly as high-pitched as Nellie's but with a wild, nervous tremolo in it.

'What am I saying to Bobby Healy?' she echoed mechanically. 'I'm saying nothing at all to him.'

'Well, don't be keeping him down there, after I waiting all day for him.'

'There's nothing wrong with his lungs anyway,' the doctor said professionally and went up the stairs. They were bare and damp. It was a lifelong grievance of Bill Enright's that the Rowes had been mean enough to take the furniture to England with them.

He was sitting up in an iron bed, and the grey afternoon

light and the white pillows threw up the brilliance of his colouring, already heightened by a touch of fever.

'What was she telling you?' he asked in his high-pitched voice – the sort of keen and unsentimental voice one would attribute in fancy to some cunning and swift-footed animal, like a fox.

'What was I telling him?' Nellie echoed boldly, feeling the doctor's authority behind her. 'I was telling him you went out with three men and two dogs and never came back to me till Friday night.'

'Ah, Bill, how often did I tell you to stick to women and cats?' the doctor said. 'What ails you now?'

'I'm bloody bad, doctor,' whinnied Bill.

'You look it,' said Bobby candidly. 'That's all right, Nellie,' he added, seeing that Nellie was proposing to examine the patient with him.

'And make a lot of noise downstairs,' said Bill after her.

Bobby gave Bill a thorough examination. So far as he could see there was nothing wrong with him but a chill, though he realized from the way Bill's mad blue eyes followed him that the man was in a panic. He wondered whether, as he sometimes did, he shouldn't give him a worse one. It was unprofessional, of course, but it was the only treatment that ever worked, and with most of his men patients he had to choose a time, before it was too late and had not yet passed from fiction to fact, when the threat of heart-disease or cirrhosis might reduce their drinking to reasonable proportions. Then the inspiration came to him like heaven opening to sinners, and he sat for some moments in silence, thinking it out. Even threats would be lost on Bill Enright. What Bill needed was a miracle, and miracles are not things to be undertaken lightly. Properly performed, a miracle might do as much good for the doctor as for Bill.

'Well, Bobby?' Bill asked, on edge with nerves.

'You're bad enough,' the doctor said gravely. 'Tell me, how long is it since you were at confession?'

Bill's rosy face turned the colour of wax, and Bobby, a kindly man, felt almost ashamed of himself.

'Is that the way it is, Bobby?' Bill asked.

'I didn't mean it like that,' the doctor said, beginning already to relent. 'But I should have a second opinion.'

'Your opinion is good enough for me, Bobby,' Bill said loyally, pouring coals of fire on Bobby. He sat up in bed and drew the clothes round him. 'Take a fag and light one for me. What the hell difference does it make? I lived my life and bred the best greyhound bitches in Europe.'

'You'll breed more,' the doctor said firmly. 'It's just that after a certain point I don't like my patients not to see a priest. It gets me a bad name. Will I go to the Canon for you?'

'The Half-Gent?' Bill said indignantly. 'You will not.'

'I know he has an unfortunate manner,' the doctor admitted sadly. 'But I can easy bring you someone else.'

'Ah, what the hell do I want with any of them?' Bill asked angrily. 'They're all the same. Money, money, money! They never think of anything else.'

'Ah, I wouldn't say that, Bill,' the doctor said thoughtfully pacing the room, his wrinkled old face as grey as his homespun suit. 'I hope you won't think I'm intruding. I'm talking as a friend.'

'I know you mean it well, Bobby,' Bill said with a sturdiness that went to the doctor's heart.

'But you see, Bill, I feel you need a different sort of priest altogether. Of course, I'm not criticizing the Canon, but after all, he's only a secular. I suppose you never had a chat with a Jesuit?'

He asked this with an innocent air as though he didn't know that the one thing a secular priest dreads after the Devil himself is a Jesuit, and that Jesuits were particularly hateful to the Canon, who considered that as much intellect and authority as his flock required were centred in himself.

'Never,' said Bill.

'They're a very cultured order,' said the doctor.

'What the hell do I want with a Jesuit?' Bill cried. 'A drop of drink and bit of skirt – what harm is there in that?'

'Oh, none in the world, Bill' agreed Bobby. ' 'Tisn't as if you were ever a bad-living man.'

'I wasn't,' Bill said with unexpected self-pity. 'I was a good friend to anyone I liked.'

'And you know the Canon would take it as a personal favour if anything happened you? You won't repeat what I'm saying – I'm speaking as a friend.'

'You are, Bobby,' said Bill, his voice hardening under the injustice of it. 'You're speaking like a Christian. Nothing would please that fellow better than to say I was down in hell. I see that clearly now. You're right. That's the way to thwart him. I could even leave the Jesuits a few pounds for Masses, Bobby,' he went on with childlike enthusiasm. 'That would really break his heart.'

'Ah, I wouldn't go as far as that, Bill,' the doctor said with some alarm. His was a delicate undertaking, and Bill was altogether too apt a pupil for his taste.

'No, but that's what you mean, Bobby,' Bill said, showing his teeth. 'And you're right as usual. Bring whoever you like and I'll let him talk. What the hell harm can it do me anyway?'

The doctor went downstairs and found Nellie waiting for him.

'I'm running over to Aharna for a priest, Nellie,' he whispered. 'You might get things ready for him while I'm away.'

'And is that the way it is?' she asked, growing pale.

'Ah, he'll be all right now. Just leave him to me,' the doctor said, squeezing her arm.

He drove off to Aharna where an ancient bishop called McGinty, whose name was remembered in clerical circles only with sorrow, had permitted the Jesuits to establish a house. There he had a friend called Father Finnegan, a stocky, middle-aged man with a tight mouth and clumps of white hair in his ears. It is not to be supposed that the doctor told him all that was in his mind, or that Father Finnegan believed he did, but they were old friends, and Father Finnegan knew that this was an occasion.

As they drove up the avenue, Nellie rushed out to meet them.

'What is it, Nellie?' the doctor asked anxiously. He could not help dreading that at the last moment Bill would play a trick on him and die of shock.

'He's gone mad, doctor,' she replied reproachfully, as though she hadn't thought Bobby would do a thing like that to her.

'When did he go mad?' Bobby asked.

'When he saw me putting up the altar in the room. He thrown a glass at me. Now he's after barricading the door and says he'll shoot the first one that tries to get in.'

'That's quite all right, my dear young lady,' Father Finnegan said comfortingly. 'Sick people often take turns like that.'

'Has he a gun, Nellie?' Bobby asked cautiously.

'Did you ever know him without one?' retorted Nellie.

The doctor, who was of a timid disposition, was impressed by the Jesuit's quiet courage. While Bobby knocked on the bedroom door, Father Finnegan stood beside it, his hands behind his back and his head bowed in meditation.

'Who's there?' cried Bill.

'It's me, Bill,' the doctor said soothingly.

'I'm not seeing anyone,' shouted Bill. 'I'm too sick.'

'One moment, doctor,' Father Finnegan said, putting his shoulder to the door. The barricade gave way and they went in. One glance was enough to show the doctor that Bill had had time to panic. He hadn't a gun, but this was the only thing lacking to remind Bobby of Two-Gun Joe's last stand. He was sitting well up in bed, supported on his elbows, his head craned forward, while his blue eyes flashed unseeingly from the priest to Bobby and from Bobby to the improvised altar. Bobby was sadly afraid that Bill was going to disappoint him. He felt he had been too optimistic. You might as well have tried to convert something in the zoo.

'I'm Father Finnegan, Mr Enright,' the Jesuit said, holding out his hand.

'I didn't send for you,' snapped Bill.

'I appreciate that, Mr Enright,' said the priest. 'But any friend of Dr Healy is a friend of mine. Won't you shake hands?'

'I don't mind,' whinnied Bill, letting him partake slightly of a limp paw but without looking at him. 'I warn you I'm not a religious sort of bloke, though. Anyone that thinks I'm not a hard nut to crack is in for a surprise.'

'If I went in for cracking nuts I'd say the same,' Father Finnegan said gamely. 'You look well able to protect yourself.'

Bill gave a harsh snort, indicating how much he could say on that score if he felt like it, and his eyes continued to wander sightlessly like a mirror in a child's hand, but Bobby felt the priest had said the right thing. He closed the door softly behind him and went down to the drawing room. The six windows opened on three landscapes. The lowing of distant cows pleased him. Then he swore and threw open the door to the hall. Nellie was sitting snugly on the stairs with her ear cocked. He beckoned her down.

'What is it, doctor?' she asked in surprise.

'Bring in a lamp. And don't forget the priest will want his supper.'

' 'Tisn't listening you thought I was?' she cried indignantly.

'No,' said Bobby dryly. 'You looked as if you were joining in the devotions.'

'Joining in the devotions,' she cried. 'I'm up since six, waiting hand and foot on him, with the result that I dropped down in a dead weakness on the stairs. Would you believe that now?'

'I would not,' said Bobby.

'You would not?' she said. 'Jesus!' she added after a moment. 'I'll bring you the lamp,' she said in a tone of defeat.

Nearly an hour passed before there was any sound from upstairs. Then Father Finnegan came down, rubbing his hands briskly and saying the nights were turning cold. Bobby found a lamp lit in the bedroom and the patient lying with one arm under his head.

'How are you feeling now, Bill?' the doctor asked.

'Fine, Bobby,' said Bill in a tone of great satisfaction. 'I'm feeling grand. You were right about the priest, Bobby.

You're always right. I'll say that for you. I was a fool to bother my head with the other fellow. He's not educated at all, Bobby, not compared with this man.'

'I thought you'd like him,' said Bobby.

'Damn it, I like a fellow to know his job, Bobby,' Bill said in the tone of one expert appraising another. 'There's nothing like the bit of education. I should have had more of it myself. I wish I met that priest sooner.' The wild blue eyes came to rest hauntingly on the doctor's face. 'I feel the better of it already, Bobby. I feel like a new man. What sign would that be?'

'I dare say it's the excitement,' Bobby said, giving nothing away. 'I'll have another look at you.'

'What's that she's frying, Bobby? Sausages and bacon?'

'I suppose so,' said the doctor, who suffered from dyspepsia and knew what the rural cookery ran to.

'There's nothing I'm so fond of,' Bill said wistfully. 'Bobby, could I have just a mouthful? My stomach feels as if it was sandpapered.'

'I suppose you could,' the doctor said grudgingly. 'But tea is all you can have with it.'

'Hah!' Bill crowed bitterly. 'That's all I'm ever going to be let have if I live to be as old as Methuselah. But I'm not complaining, Bobby. I'm a man of my word. Oh, God, yes.'

'Don't tell me you took the pledge, Bill!' the doctor said doubtfully.

'Christ, Bobby,' said the patient, giving a wild heave in the bed, 'I took the whole bloody book, cover and all ... God forgive me for swearing!' he added piously. 'He made me promise to marry the Screech,' he said with a look that challenged the doctor to laugh if he didn't value his life.

'And why wouldn't you if you wanted to?' asked the doctor.

'How sure he is I'll have him!' Nellie bawled cheerfully, showing her moony face at the door.

'That's why, Bobby,' Bill said without rancour. 'It have my nerves on edge. I'm a man that likes to keep his mind to himself.'

'Go on, Nellie!' said the doctor. 'I'm having a look at Bill

'... You had a trying day of it,' he added as she went out. He sat on the bed and took Bill's wrist. Then he stuck a thermometer in his throat, flashed a torch in his eyes and examined his throat while Bill looked at him with a hypnotized glare.

'Begor, Bill, I wouldn't say but you were right,' the doctor said with a laugh that might have suggested surprise and embarrassment. 'I'd almost say you were a shade better.'

'A shade?' said Bill, beginning to do physical exercises for him. 'Look at that, Bobby! I couldn't do that before. That's not what I call a shade. It came over me while he was talking. I call that a blooming miracle.'

'When you've seen as much as I have, you won't believe so much in miracles,' the doctor said sourly. At this stage he did not want Bill to go out and get double pneumonia on him, all to prove that a Jesuit had cured him when a doctor had given him up. 'Take a couple of these tablets, and I'll have another look at you in the morning.'

He was almost depressed as he went downstairs. It was too easy altogether. The most up-to-date treatments were wasted on Bobby's patients. What they all secretly wanted was to be rubbed with three pebbles from a Holy Well.

'Well, on the whole, Dr Healy,' Father Finnegan said as they drove off, 'that was a very satisfactory evening.'

'I'd say it was,' Bobby said guardedly. He had no intention of telling his friend exactly how satisfactory it was.

'And people do make the most extraordinary rallies after the sacraments,' Father Finnegan went on, and Bobby saw that it wasn't even necessary to explain to him. Educated men can understand one another without such embarrassing admissions. His own conscience was quite clear. A little religion wouldn't do Bill the least bit of harm. He felt that the priest's conscience wasn't troubling him much either. He wasn't especially required to love seculars, and, even without a miracle, Bill's conversion would throw the parish wide open to the order. *With* a miracle, testified to by a medical man, every old woman, male and female, for miles around, would be calling for a Jesuit.

'They do,' Bobby said wonderingly. ' 'Tis a thing you'd often notice.'

'But I'm afraid, Dr Healy, that the Canon won't like it,' the Jesuit added candidly.

'He won't,' the doctor said as though the idea had only just occurred to him. 'I'm afraid he won't like it at all.'

He was an honest man who gave credit where credit was due, and he knew it wasn't only the money – a couple of hundred a year at least – that would upset the Canon. It was the thought that under his very nose a miracle had been worked on one of his own parishioners by a member of the hated Jesuit order. Clerics, he knew, are as cruel as small boys. The Canon would not be allowed to forget the Jesuit miracle the longest day he lived.

But for the future he'd let Bobby alone.

The Common Chord (1947)

THE FRYING PAN

Father Fogarty's only friends in Kilmulpeter were the Whittons. Whitton, the schoolteacher, had been to the seminary with Fogarty, and like him, intended to be a priest, but when the time came for him to take the vow of celibacy, he had contracted scruples of conscience and married the most important of them. Fogarty, who had known her too, had agreed that there was justification for that particular scruple, and now, in this lonely place where chance had thrown them together again, she formed the real centre of what little social life he had.

With Tom Whitton he had a quiet friendship based on exchanges of opinion about books and wireless talks, but he felt that Whitton didn't really like him. When they went to the races together, Fogarty felt that Whitton disapproved of having to put on bets for him and believed that priests should not bet at all. Like other outsiders, he knew perfectly what priests should do, without the necessity for doing it himself. He was sometimes savage in the things he said about the parish priest, old Father Whelan. On the other hand, he had a ready wit, and Fogarty enjoyed retelling his cracks against the cloth. Men as intelligent as Whitton were rare in country schools, and soon he, too, would grow stupid and wild for lack of educated society.

One evening Father Fogarty invited the Whittons to dinner to see some films he had taken at the races. Films were his latest hobby. Before that it had been fishing and shooting. Like all bachelors he had a mania for adding to his possessions, and his lumber-room was piled high with every sort of junk from chest-developers to field-glasses (these belonged to his bird-watching phase), and his library cluttered with text-books on everything from Irish history to Freudian psychology. He passed from craze to craze, each the key to the universe.

He sprang up at the knock, and found Una at the door, all in furs, her shoulders about her ears, her big, bony, masculine face blue with cold. She had an amiable monkey-grin. Tom, a handsome man, was tall and self-conscious. He had greying hair, brown eyes, a prominent jaw, and was quiet-spoken in a way that concealed passion. He and Una disagreed a lot about how the children should be brought up. He thought she spoiled them.

'Come in, let ye, come in!' cried Fogarty, showing the way into his warm study, with its roaring turf-fire, deep leather chairs, and the Raphael print over the mantelpiece – a typical bachelor's room. 'You're perished, Una!' he said with concern, holding her hand a moment longer than was necessary. 'What'll you have to drink?'

'Whi-hi-hi—' stammered Una excitedly, her eyes beginning to pop. 'I can't say the bloody word.'

'Call it malt,' said Fogarty, spinning on his heel towards the sideboard.

'That's enough! That's enough!' she cried laughingly, snatching the glass from him. 'You'll send me home on my ear, and then I'll hear about it from this fellow.'

'Whiskey, Tom?'

'Whiskey, Jerry,' Whitton said quietly with a quick friendly glance. He kept his head very still and used his eyes a lot instead.

Meanwhile Una, unabashably inquisitive, was making the tour of the room with the glass in her hand, to see if there wasn't something new in it. There usually was.

'Is this new, father?' she asked, halting before a pleasant eighteenth-century print.

'Ten bob,' the priest said promptly. 'Wasn't it a bargain?'

'I couldn't say. What is it?'

'The old courthouse in town.'

'Go on!' said Una.

Whitton walked over and studied the print closely. 'That place is gone these fifty years and I never saw a picture of it,' he said. 'This is a bargain all right.'

'I'd say so,' Fogarty said with quiet pride.

'And what's the sheet for?' asked Una, poking at a table-cloth pinned between the windows.

'That's not a sheet, woman!' Fogarty exclaimed. 'For God's sake don't be displaying your ignorance.'

'Oh, I know,' she cried girlishly. 'For the pictures. I'd for-gotten about them. That's grand!'

Then Bella, a coarse, good-looking country girl an-nounced dinner, and the curate, with a self-conscious, boy-ish swagger, led them into the dining room, which was even more ponderous than the study. Everything in it was large, heavy and dark.

'And now, what'll ye drink?' he asked over his shoulder, studying his array of bottles. 'There's some damn good Bur-gundy – 'pon my soul, 'tis great!'

'How much did it cost?' Whitton asked with poker-faced humour. 'The only way I have of identifying wine is by the price.'

'Eight bob a bottle,' Fogarty replied at once, without per-ceiving the joke.

'That's a very good price,' said Whitton with a nod. 'We'll have some of that.'

'You can take a couple of bottles home with you,' said Fogarty, who, in the warmth of his heart, was always wanting to give his treasures away. 'The last two dozen he had – wasn't I lucky?'

'You have the appetite of a canon on the income of a curate,' Whitton said in the same tone of grave humour, but Fogarty caught the scarcely perceptible note of criticism in it. He did not allow it to worry him.

'Please God, we won't always be curates,' he said sunnily.

'Bella looks after you well,' said Una when the meal was nearly over. The compliment was deserved so far as it went, though it was a man's meal rather than a woman's.

'Doesn't she though?' Fogarty exclaimed with pleasure. 'Isn't she damn good for a country girl?'

'How does she get on with Stasia?' asked Una. Stasia, Father Whelan's old housekeeper, was an affliction to the whole community.

'They don't talk. Stasia says she's an immoral woman.'

'And is she?' asked Una hopefully.

'If she's not, she's wasting her own time and my whiskey,' said Fogarty. 'She entertains Paddy Coakley in the kitchen every Saturday night while I'm hearing confessions. I told her I wouldn't keep her unless she got a boy. Aren't I right? One Stasia is enough for any parish. Father Whelan tells me I'm going too far.'

'And did you tell him to mind his own business?' Whitton asked with a penetrating look.

'I did, to be sure,' said Fogarty, who had done nothing of the kind. It was hardly the sort of thing you could say to a parish priest.

'Ignorant, interfering old fool!' Whitton said quietly, the ferocity of his sentiments belied by the mildness of his manner.

'That's only because you'd like to do the interfering yourself, love,' said Una, who frequently had to act as peacemaker between the parish priest and her husband.

'And a robber as well,' Whitton added, ignoring her. 'He's been collecting for new seats for the church for the last ten years. I'd like to know where that money is going.'

'He had a collection for repairing my roof and 'tis leaking still,' said Fogarty. 'He must be worth twenty thousand.'

'Now, that's not fair,' Una said flatly. 'You know yourself there's no harm in Father Whelan. It's only that he's sure he's going to die in the poorhouse. It's just like Bella and her boy – he has nothing more serious to worry about, and he worries about that.'

Fogarty knew there was a certain amount of truth in what Una said, and that Whelan's miserliness was more symbolic than real, but at the same time he felt in her words criticism of a different kind. Though she wasn't aware of it herself, she was implying that the priest's office made him an object of pity. He wasn't a man like anybody else, and this made her sorry for him, and, by implication, for Fogarty himself. This had to be put down.

'Still, Tom is right, Una,' he said gravely. 'It's not a question of what harm Father Whelan intends but what harm he does. Scandal is scandal, whatever the cause may be.'

Tom grunted approval, but he said no more on the subject, as though refusing to enter into argument with his wife about things she didn't understand.

They returned to the study for coffee, and Fogarty brought out the film projector. At once the censoriousness of Tom Whitton's manner dropped away, and he behaved with the new toy like a pleasant and intelligent boy of seventeen. Una, sitting by the fire with her legs crossed, watched them with amusement. Whenever they came to the priest's house, the same sort of thing was liable to happen. Once it had been a microscope, another time a chest-developer, and now they were kidding themselves that their real interest in the cinema was educational. Within a month the projector, like the microscope, would be lying in the lumber room with the rest of the junk.

Fogarty switched off the light and showed some films he had taken at the races. They were very patchy, mostly out of focus, and had to be interpreted by a running commentary, which was always a shot or two behind.

'I suppose ye wouldn't know who that is?' he asked as the film showed Una, eating a sandwich and talking excitedly and demonstratively to a couple of wild-looking country boys.

'It looks like someone from the County Club,' her husband said dryly.

'But wasn't it good?' Fogarty asked innocently, switching on the light again. 'Now, wasn't it very interesting?' He was exactly like a small boy who has performed a conjuring trick and is waiting for the applause.

'Marvellous, father,' Una said with a sly and affectionate grin.

He blushed and turned away to pour out more whiskey for them. He saw that she had noticed the pictures of herself and wasn't displeased with them. When he drove them home, she held his hand and said they had had the best evening for years – a piece of flattery so gross and uncalled for that it made her husband more tongue-tied than ever.

'Thursday, Jerry?' he said with a quick glance.

'Thursday, Tom,' said the priest.

The room looked terribly desolate after Una; the crumpled cushions, the glasses, the screen and the film projector. Everything had become frighteningly inert, while outside his window the desolate countryside had taken on even more of its supernatural animation – bogs, hills and fields, full of ghosts and shadows. He sat by the fire, wondering what his life might have been with a girl like that, all furs and scent and laughter, and two bawling, irrepressible brats upstairs. When he tiptoed up to his bedroom he remembered that there never would be children there to wake, and it seemed to him that with all the things he bought to fill his home, he was merely trying desperately to stuff the yawning holes in his own big, empty heart.

On Thursday, when he went to their house, Ita and Brendan were in bed, but refusing to sleep till he said goodnight to them – a regular ritual. While he was taking off his coat the two of them rushed to the banisters and screamed: 'We want Father Fogey.' When he went upstairs they were sitting bolt-upright in their cots, unnaturally clean, a little fat, fair-haired rowdy boy and a solemn baby girl.

'Father, will I be your alboy when I grow up?' Brendan

began at once. To be an acolyte was now his great ambition.

'You will to be sure, son,' said Fogarty. 'I wouldn't have anyone else.'

'Ladies first! Ladies first!' the baby shrieked in a frenzy. 'Will I be your alboy, father?'

'Go on!' Brendan said scornfully. 'Little girls can't be alboys, sure they can't, father?'

'I can, I can,' shrieked Ita, who in her excitement exactly resembled her mother. 'Can't I, father?'

'Ah, we'll get a dispensation for you,' Fogarty said soothingly. 'In a pair of trousers, who'd know?'

He was in a wistful frame of mind when he came downstairs again. Children would always be a worse temptation to him than women. Children were the devil, the way they got under your guard.

The house was gay and spotless. The Whittons had no fine mahogany suite like his, but Una managed to make the few coloured odds and ends seem deliberate. The ashtrays were polished, the cushions puffed up. Tom, standing before the fireplace (not to disturb the cushions, thought Fogarty), looked as though someone had held his head under a tap, and was very self-consciously wearing a new brown tie. With his greying hair plastered flat, he looked schoolboyish, sulky and resentful, as though he was contemplating ways of restoring his authority over a mutinous household. The thought crossed Fogarty's mind that he and Una had probably quarrelled over the tie. It went altogether too well with his suit.

'We want Father Fogey,' the children began to chant monotonously from the bedroom.

'Shut up!' Tom shouted back, as though glad to find an enemy to hit back at.

'We want Father Fogey,' the chant went on, but with a groan in it somewhere.

'Well, you're not going to get him. Go to sleep!'

The chant stopped. The old man was clearly in a bad humour.

'You don't mind if I drop down to a meeting tonight, Jerry?' Tom asked in his anxious, quiet way. 'I won't be much more than half an hour.'

'Not at all, Tom,' said Fogarty. 'Sure, I'll drive you.'

'No, thanks,' Whitton said with a quick smile. 'It won't take me ten minutes to get there.'

It was clear that a lot of trouble had gone into the supper, but out of sheer perversity, Whitton let on not to recognize any of the dishes. When they had drunk their coffee he rose and glanced at his watch.

'See you later, Jerry,' he said.

'Tom, you're *not* going to that meeting?' Una asked appealingly.

'I tell you I have to.'

'And I met Mick Mahoney this afternoon, and he said there was no need for you to come.'

'A fat lot Mick Mahoney knows about it!'

'I told him to say that Father Fogarty would be here and you wouldn't come,' she went on desperately, fighting for the success of her evening.

'Then you had no business to do it,' Whitton said angrily, and even Fogarty realized that she had gone the wrong way about it. He began to feel uncomfortable. 'If they come to some damn fool decision when I'm not there, I'll have to take the responsibility for it.'

'If you're late you'd better knock,' she sang out gaily to cover his rudeness. 'Will we go into the sitting room, father?' she asked over-eagerly. 'I'll be with you in two minutes. There are fags on the mantelpiece, and you know where to find the whi-hi-hi—blast that word!'

Fogarty lit a cigarette and sat down. He was feeling very uncomfortable. Whitton was an uncouth and irritable bastard and always had been. He heard Una upstairs and someone turned on the tap in the bathroom. 'Bloody brute!' he thought indignantly. There had been no call for Whitton to insult her before a guest. Why couldn't he have finished his quarrelling while they were alone? The tap stopped and he waited, listening. You could hear everything in that cheap modern house. He was a warm-hearted man and he could not bear the thought of her alone and miserable upstairs. He went quietly up the stairs and stood on the landing. 'Una!' he called softly, afraid of waking the children. There was a light in the bedroom; the door was ajar and he pushed it in. Una was sitting at the end of the bed with a handkerchief in her hand and grinned up dolefully at him.

'Sorry for the whine, father,' she said, making an attempt to smile. Then, with the street-urchin's humour he found so attractive – 'Can I have a loan of your shoulder, please?'

'What the blazes ails Tom?' he asked, sitting beside her.

'He – he's jealous,' she stammered, and began to weep again with her head on his chest. He put his arm about her and patted her awkwardly.

'Jealous?' he asked incredulously, turning over in his mind the half dozen men Una could meet at the best of times. 'Who is he jealous of?'

'He's jealous of you,' she said, sobbing.

'Me?' Fogarty exclaimed, and grew red, thinking of how he had given himself away with his pictures. 'He must be mad! I never gave him any cause for jealousy.'

'Oh, I know he's completely unreasonable,' she said. 'He always was.'

'But you didn't say anything to him, did you?' Fogarty asked anxiously. 'About me, I mean?'

'Oh, he doesn't know about that,' Una replied frantically. 'That's not what he's jealous about. He doesn't give a snap of his fingers about me that way.'

And Fogarty realized that in the simplest way in the world he had been brought to admit to a married woman that he was in love with her and she to imply that she didn't mind, without an indelicate word on either side. Clearly, these things sometimes happened more innocently than he had ever imagined. That made him more embarrassed than ever.

'But what is he jealous of, so?' he asked.

'He's jealous of you because you're a priest,' she said, laughing through her tears. 'Surely, you saw that.'

'I certainly didn't. It never even crossed my mind. It's rather a queer thing for a man to be jealous about.'

Yet at the same time Fogarty wondered if this might not be the reason for the censoriousness he sometimes felt in

Whitton against his harmless extravagances.

'But he's hardly ever out of your house, and he's always borrowing your religious books, and talking theology and Church history to you,' she said, shaking her head at him wonderingly. 'And he has shelves of them already here – look, will you? Look at that bookcase! In my bedroom! That's why he hates Father Whelan. Don't you see, Jerry,' she said, calling him by his Christian name for the first time, 'you have all the things he wants.'

'I have?' Fogarty asked incredulously. 'What things?'

'Oh, how do I know?' she replied contemptuously, relegating them to the same class as Father Whelan's bank balance and his own film camera. 'Respect and responsibility and freedom from family worries, I suppose.'

'He's welcome to them,' Fogarty said with a wry laugh. 'What's that the advertisements say? – owner having no further use for same. I'd say he was the one who had everything.'

'Oh, I know,' she said with another shrug, and he saw that from the beginning she had realized how he felt about her, and liked him too, and been sorry. He was sure there was some contradiction here between her almost inordinate piety and her calm acceptance of his feeling for her – something that was exclusively feminine.

'It's a change to be with a man who likes you,' she added with a mawkish smile.

'Ah, now, Una, that's not true,' he protested gravely, the priest in him getting the upper hand of the lover, who still had a considerable amount to learn. 'You only fancy that.'

'I don't, Jerry,' she said with bitter emphasis. 'It's always been the same from the first month we were married – always, always, always! I was a bloody fool to marry him at all.'

'Even so, you know he's still fond of you,' Fogarty said manfully, doing his duty by his friend with schoolboy gravity. 'That's only his way.'

'It's not, Jerry,' she said obstinately. 'He wanted to be a priest and I stopped him.'

'But you didn't.'

'That's how he looks at it. He thinks I tempted him. Maybe I did. I paid dear for it.'

'And damn glad he was to fall!'

'But he *did* fall, Jerry, and that's what he'll never forgive me for. In his heart he despises me, and he despises himself for not being able to do without me.'

'But what does he despise himself for?' cried Fogarty. 'That's what I can't understand.'

'Because he despises all women, and he wants to be independent of us all. He has to teach to keep a home for me, and he doesn't want to teach. He wants to say Mass and hear confessions, and be God Almighty for seven days of the week.'

Fogarty couldn't grasp it, but he realized that there was something in what she said, and that Whitton was probably a lonely frustrated man who felt he was forever excluded from the only world that interested him.

'I don't understand it,' he said explosively. 'Damn it, it's unnatural.'

'It's unnatural to you because you have it, Jerry,' she said. 'I used to think Tom was unnatural too, but now I'm beginning to think there are more spoiled priests in the world than ever went into seminaries. I don't mean people like you. You're different. You could never be as inhuman as that. But you see, Jerry, I'm a constant reproach to him. He wants to make love to me once a month, and even then, he's ashamed of it . . . I can talk like this to you because you're a priest.'

'You can,' Fogarty said, though he wished she wouldn't. Anybody else but she! But she was so full of her grievance that she didn't even notice the pain she caused him.

'And even when he does, he manages to make me feel that I'm doing it all.'

'And why shouldn't you?' asked Fogarty angrily.

'Because it's a sin!' she said tempestuously.

'Who says it's a sin?'

'He thinks it's a sin. He's like a bear with a sore head for days after it. Don't you see, Jerry, to him it's never anything only adultery, and he goes away and curses himself because he hasn't the strength to resist it.'

'Adultery?' repeated Fogarty, the familiar word knocking at his conscience as though it were Tom Whitton himself at the door.

'Whatever you call it,' Una rushed on. 'It's always adultery, adultery, adultery, and I'm always a bad woman and he always wants to show God it wasn't him but me, and I'm sick to death of it. I want to get a bit of fun out of going to bed with a man, and feel like a respectable married woman after it. I feel respectable with you, though I suppose I shouldn't.' She looked in the mirror of the dressing table and her face fell. 'Oh, Lord!' she sighed. 'I don't look very respectable, do I? ... I'll be down in two minutes now, Jerry,' she said eagerly.

'You're grand,' he muttered thickly.

As he went downstairs he was very thoughtful. He heard Tom's key in the latch and looked at himself in the mirror over the fireplace. He heard Tom's step in the hall, and it sounded in his ears as it had never sounded before, like that of a man carrying a burden too great for him. He realized that he had never before seen Whitton as he really was, a man at war with his animal nature, longing for some high, solitary existence of the intellect and imagination. And he knew that the three of them, Whitton, Una and himself, would die as they had lived, their desires unsatisfied.

The Common Chord (1947)

THE MAN OF THE HOUSE

As a kid I was as good as gold so long as I could concentrate. Concentration, that was always my weakness, in school and everywhere else. Once I was diverted from whatever I was doing, I was lost.

It was like that when Mother got ill. I remember it well; how I waked that morning and heard the strange cough in the kitchen below. From that very moment I knew something was wrong. I dressed and went down. She was sitting in a little wickerwork chair before the fire, holding her side. She had made an attempt to light the fire but it had gone against her.

'What's wrong, Mum?' I said.

'The sticks were wet and the fire started me coughing,' she said, trying to smile, though I could see she was doubled up with pain.

'I'll light the fire and you go back to bed,' I said.

'Ah, how can I, child?' she said. 'Sure, I have to go to work.'

'You couldn't work like that,' I said. 'Go on up to bed now and I'll bring up your breakfast.'

It's funny about women, the way they'll take orders from anything in trousers, even if it is only ten.

'If you could make a cup of tea for yourself I'd be all right in an hour or two,' she said, and shuffled feebly upstairs. I went with her, supporting her arm, and when she reached the bed she collapsed. I knew then she must be feeling bad. I got more sticks – she was so economical that she never used enough – and I soon had the fire roaring and the kettle on. I made her toast as well: I was always a great believer in buttered toast.

I thought she looked at the cup of tea rather doubtfully.

'Is that all right?' I asked.

'You wouldn't have a sup of boiling water left?' she asked.

' 'Tis too strong,' I said, trying to keep the disappointment out of my voice. 'I'll pour half of it away. I can never remember about tea.'

'I hope you won't be late for school,' she said anxiously.

'I'm not going to school,' I said. 'I'll get you your tea now and do the messages after.'

She didn't complain at my not going to school. It was just as I said: orders were all she wanted. I washed up the breakfast things, then I washed myself and went up to her with the shopping basket, a piece of paper, and a lead pencil.

'I'll do the messages if you'll write them down,' I said. 'I suppose I'll go to Mrs Slattery first.'

'Tell her I'll be in tomorrow, without fail.'

'Write down Mrs Slattery,' I said firmly. 'Would I get the doctor?'

'Indeed, you'll do nothing of the kind,' Mother said anxiously. 'He'd only want to send me to hospital. They're all alike. You could ask the chemist to give you a good strong cough bottle.'

'Write it down,' I said, remembering my own weakness. 'If I haven't it written down I might forget it. And put "strong" in big letters. What will I get for the dinner? Eggs?'

That was really only swank, because eggs were the only thing I could cook, but the mother told me to get sausages as well in case she was able to get up.

It was a lovely sunny morning. I called first on Mrs Slattery, whom my mother worked for, to tell her she wouldn't be in. Mrs Slattery was a woman I didn't like much. She had a big broad face that needed big broad features, but all she had was narrow little eyes and a thin, pointed nose that seemed to get lost in the width of her face.

'She said she'll try to get in tomorrow, but I don't know will I let her up,' I said airily.

'I wouldn't if she wasn't well, Gus,' she said, and gave me a penny.

By this time pride was going a little to my head. That is another weakness of mine, pride. I went by the school and stood opposite it for a full ten minutes, staring. The schoolhouse and the sloping yard were like a picture, except for the chorus of poor sufferers through the open windows, and a glimpse of Danny Delaney's bald pate as he did sentry-go before the front door with his cane wriggling like a tail behind his back. That was nice. It was nice too to be chatting to the assistants in the shops and telling them about Mother's cough. I made it out a bit worse to make a better story of it, but all the time I had a hope that when I reached home she'd be up so that we could have sausages for dinner. I hated boiled eggs, and, anyway, I was beginning to feel the strain of my responsibilities.

But when I got home it was to find Minnie Ryan with her. Minnie was an old maid, gossipy and pious, but very knowledgeable.

'How are you feeling now, Mum?' I asked.

'Oh, I'm grand,' she said with a smile.

'She won't be able to get up today, though,' Minnie said firmly.

'I'll pour you out your cough-bottle so, and make you a cup of tea,' I said, concealing my disappointment and a certain resentment of Minnie Ryan, who could have minded her own business.

'Wisha, I'll do that for you, child,' she said meekly, getting up.

'Ah, you needn't mind, Miss Ryan,' I said nobly. 'I can manage all right.'

'Isn't he great?' I heard Minnie say in a low, wondering voice as I went downstairs. She expressed my own sentiments exactly.

'Minnie, he's the best a woman ever reared,' whispered my mother.

'Why, then, there aren't many like him,' Minnie said bleakly. 'The most of the children that's going are more like savages than Christians.'

In the afternoon Mother wanted me to go out and play, but remembering my weakness, I didn't go far. I knew if I once went a certain distance I should drift towards the Glen, with the barrack drill-field perched on a cliff above it; the rifle-range below, and below that again, the mill-pond and mill-stream running through a wooded gorge – the Rockies, Himalayas, or Highlands, according to your mood. If I once went in that direction, the Lord alone knew when I should come back, and then I should be among the children Minnie Ryan disapproved of who were more like savages than Christians.

Evening came; the street lamps were lit, and the paper boy went crying up the road. I bought a paper, lit the lamp in the kitchen and the candle in the bedroom, and read the police court news to Mother. I knew it was the piece she liked best. I wasn't very quick about it, because I was only at words of one syllable, but she didn't seem to mind.

Later Minnie Ryan came again, and as she left I went to the front door with her. She looked grave.

'If she's not better in the morning I think I'd get a doctor to her, Gus,' she said quietly.

'Why?' I asked in alarm. 'Is she worse?'

'Ah, no, only I'd be frightened of the old pneumonia,' she said, giving her shawl a nervous tug.

'But wouldn't he send her to hospital, Miss Ryan?' I asked. To us, of course, the hospital almost meant the end.

'Ah, he mightn't,' she said without conviction. 'He could give her a good bottle. And even if he did send her to hospital, God between us and all harm, 'twould be better than neglecting it . . . If you had a drop of whiskey you could give it to her hot with a squeeze of lemon.'

'I'll get it,' I said at once.

Mother did not want the whiskey; she said we couldn't afford it, but I felt it might cost less than hospital and all its horrors, and I wouldn't let her put me off.

I had never been in a public-house before, and the crowd inside frightened me.

'Hullo, my old flower,' said one tall man, grinning diabolically at me. 'It must be ten years since I saw you last. One minute now – wasn't it in South Africa?'

I was never in South Africa, so I knew the man must be drunk. My pal, Bob Connell, boasted to me once how he had asked a drunk man like that for a half-crown and the man gave it to him. I was always trying to work up courage to do the same, but even then I hadn't the nerve.

'It was not,' I said. 'I want half a glass of whiskey for my mother.'

'Oh, the thundering ruffian!' the man said, clapping his hands and looking at me with astonished eyes. 'Pretending 'tis for his mother, and he the most notorious boozer in Cape Town!'

'I am not,' I said, on the verge of tears. 'And 'tis for my mother. She's sick.'

'Leave the child alone, Johnny!' the barmaid said. 'Don't you hear him say his mother is sick?'

Mother fell asleep after the hot whiskey, but I couldn't rest, wondering how the man in the public-house could think I was in South Africa, and blaming myself a lot for not asking him for the half-crown. A half-crown would come in very handy if the mother was really sick, because we never had more than a couple of shillings in the house. When I did fall asleep I was wakened again by her coughing, and when I went in, she was rambling in her speech, and didn't recognize me at first. That frightened me more than anything else.

When she was no better next morning in spite of the whiskey, I was bitterly disappointed. After I had given her her breakfast I went to see Minnie Ryan, and she came and talked to Mother for a few minutes.

'I'd get the doctor at once, Gus,' she said when she came downstairs. 'I'll stop with her while you're out.'

To get the doctor I had first to go to the house of an under-taker who was a Poor Law Guardian to get a ticket to show we couldn't pay. The Poor Law Guardian was very good about that, because afterwards he was sure of the funeral. Then I had to rush back to get the house ready, and prepare a basin of water, soap and a towel for the doctor to wash his hands.

He didn't come until after dinner. He was a fat, slow-moving, loud-voiced man with a grey moustache and the reputation of being 'the cleverest doctor in Cork if only he'd mind himself'. From the way he looked, he hadn't been minding himself much that morning.

'How are you going to get this?' he growled, sitting on the edge of the bed with his prescription pad. 'The only place open now is the North Dispensary.'

'I'll go, doctor,' I said at once.

' 'Tis a long way,' he said doubtfully. 'Do you think you'll be able to find it?'

'Oh, I'll find it,' I said confidently.

'Isn't he a great help to you?' he said to Mother.

'The best in the world, doctor,' she sighed with a long look at me.

'That's right,' he told me cunningly. 'Look after your

mother while you can. She'll be the best for you in the long run ... We don't mind them when we have them,' he said to Mother, and I could have sworn he was crying. 'Then we spend the rest of our lives regretting them.'

I didn't think he could be a very good doctor, because, after all my trouble, he never washed his hands, but I was prepared to overlook that because he had said nothing about the hospital.

The road to the dispensary led uphill through a poor and thickly-populated neighbourhood to the military barrack, which was perched on the hilltop, and then descended between high walls till it suddenly almost disappeared over the edge of the hill and degenerated into a stony pathway flanked on one side by red-brick council houses and on the other by a wide common with an astounding view of the city. From this the city looked more like the backcloth of a theatre than a real place. The pathway dropped away to the bank of a stream where a brewery stood; and from the brewery, far beneath, the opposite hillside, a murmuring honeycomb of factory chimneys and houses, where noises came to you, dissociated and ghostlike, rose steeply to the gently-rounded hilltop from which a limestone spire and a purple sandstone tower mounted into the clouds. It was so wide and bewildering a view that it was never all lit up at the same time. Sunlight wandered across it as across a prairie, picking out a line of roofs with a brightness like snow, or delving into the depth of some tunnel-like street and outlining in shadow the figures of carts and straining horses.

I felt exalted, a voyager, a heroic figure. I made up my mind to spend the penny Mrs Slattery had given me on a candle to the Blessed Virgin in the cathedral on the hilltop for my mother's recovery. A fellow couldn't expect much attention lighting candles in a small parish church.

The dispensary was a squalid hallway with a bench to one side and a window like a ticket office at the end. There was a little girl with a green plaid shawl about her shoulders sitting on the bench. She gave me a quick look and I saw that her eyes were green as well. For years after, whenever a girl looked at me like that, I hid. I knew by that time what it meant. I knocked at the office and a seedy, angry-looking man banged up the wooden screen. Without waiting to hear what I was trying to say he grabbed bottle and prescription and banged the shutter down again. I waited a minute and then lifted my hand to knock again.

'You'll have to wait, little boy,' the girl said hastily.

'Why will I have to wait?' I asked.

'He have to make it up,' she explained. 'He might be half an hour at it. You might as well sit down.'

As she obviously knew how to behave in a place like that, I did what she had told me.

'Where are you from?' she asked, dropping the shawl, which she held in front of her mouth exactly the way I'd seen old women hold it. 'I live in Blarney Lane.'

'I live beyond the barrack,' I said.

'And who's the bottle for?'

'My mother.'

'What's wrong with your mother?'

'She have a cough.'

'She might have consumption,' the girl said cheerfully. 'That's what my sister that died last year had. My other sister has to have tonics. That's what I'm waiting for. Is it nice up where ye live?'

I told her about the Glen, and she told me about the river up Sunday's Well way. It seemed a nicer place altogether than ours, as she described it. She was a pleasant, talkative little girl, and I never noticed the time passing. Suddenly the shutter went up and a bottle was banged on the counter.

'Dooley!' said the man, and the shutter went down again.

'That's mine,' said the little girl. 'My name is Nora Dooley. Yours won't be ready for a long time yet. Is it red or black?'

'I don't know,' I said. 'I never got it before.'

'Black ones is better,' she said. 'Red is more for hacking coughs.'

'I have a penny,' I said. 'I'm going to get sweets.'

I had decided that after all I didn't need to light a candle. I felt sure Mother would be all right soon, anyway, and it seemed a pity to waste the money like that.

When I got the bottle, it was black. The little girl and I sat on the steps of the infirmary and ate the sweets I had bought. At the end of the lane was the limestone spire of Shandon; all along it young trees overhung the high, hot walls, and the sun, when it came out in hot, golden blasts behind us, threw our linked shadows on to the road.

'Give us a taste of your bottle, little boy,' said the girl.

'Can't you have a taste of your own?' I said.

'Ah, you couldn't drink mine,' she said. 'Tonics is all awful. Try it and see.'

I did, and I spat it out hastily. It was awful, all right. But after that, I couldn't do less than let her taste mine. She took a long drink out of it, and this alarmed me.

'That's beautiful,' she said. 'That's like my sister that died used to get. I love cough bottles.'

I tried it, and saw she was right in a way. It was very sweet and sticky, like treacle.

'Give us another slug,' she said.

'I will not,' I said in alarm. 'What am I going to do with it now?'

'All you have to do is put water in it out of a pump. That's what I used to do, and nobody ever noticed.'

I couldn't refuse her. Mother was far away, and I was swept from anchorage into an unfamiliar world of spires, towers, trees, steps and little girls who liked cough bottles. Then I began to panic. I saw that even if you put water into it, you could not conceal the fact that it wasn't the same.

'What am I going to do now?' I said miserably.

'Ah, finish it and say the cork fell out,' she said lightly, as if surprised at my innocence. I believed her, but as I put down the empty bottle I remembered my mother sick and the Blessed Virgin slighted, and I knew I could never tell a lie the way she could. I knew, too, that she didn't care. She was through with me now. It was my cough bottle she had been after all the time. I began to weep despairingly.

'What ails you?' she said impatiently.

'My mother is sick, and you're after drinking her medicine, and now, if she dies, 'twill be my fault,' I said.

'Ah, what old nonsense you have!' she said contemptuously. 'No one ever died of a cough. All you have to say is that the cork fell out – 'tis a thing that might happen to anyone.'

'And I promised to light a candle to the Blessed Virgin, and I spent it on sweets for you,' I cried, and went away up the road, sobbing and clutching my empty bottle. She looked after me curiously, I noticed, but she didn't even follow me. I was well paid out for my folly. Now I had only one hope – a miracle. I went into the cathedral to the shrine of the Blessed Virgin, and promised her a candle with the next penny I got if only she made Mother better by the time I got home. I looked at her face carefully in the candlelight, but I couldn't make much out of it. Then I went miserably home. All the light had gone out of the day, and the echoing hillside had become a vast, alien, cruel world. Besides, I felt terribly sick. It struck me that I might even die myself. In one way that would be a great ease to me.

When I reached home, the silence of the kitchen and the sight of the empty grate told me at once that my prayers had not been heard: Mother was still sick and in bed. I began to howl.

'Wisha, what is it at all, child?' Mother cried anxiously from upstairs.

'I lost the medicine,' I bellowed from the foot of the stairs, and then dashed blindly up to bury my face in the bed-clothes.

'Ah, wisha, wisha, if that's all that's a trouble to you, you poor misfortunate child!' she cried in relief, running her hand through my hair. 'I was afraid you were lost. Is anything the matter?' she added anxiously. 'You feel hot.'

'I drank the medicine,' I bawled, and buried my face again.

'And if you did itself, what harm?' she murmured. 'You poor child, going all that way by yourself, without a proper dinner or anything! Why wouldn't you? Take off your clothes and lie down now, till you're better.'

She rose, put on her slippers and overcoat, and unlaced my shoes. Even before she finished I was asleep. Whatever was in the medicine, I couldn't keep my eyes open. I didn't hear her go out, but some time later I felt a cool hand on my forehead, and saw Minnie Ryan peering down at me.

'Ah, 'tis nothing, woman,' she said, more in amusement than anything else. 'He'll sleep it off by morning. Well, aren't they the devil! God knows, you'd never be up to them! And, indeed and indeed, Mrs Sullivan, you're the one that should be in bed.'

I knew all that. I knew it was her judgement on me. I was only another of those who were more like savages than Christians; I was no good as a nurse, no good to anyone at all. I accepted it meekly. But when Mother came up to the bedroom with her evening paper, and sat reading by the bed, I knew the miracle had happened all right. Somebody had cured her.

Travellers' Samples (1951)

MY FIRST PROTESTANT

It was when I was doing a line with Maire Daly that I first came to know Winifred Jackson. She was my first Protestant. There were a number of them in our locality, but they kept to themselves. The Jacksons were no exception. Winifred's father was a bank manager, a tall, thin, weary-looking man, and her mother a chubby, pious woman who had a lot to do with religious bazaars. They had one son, Ernest, a medical student who was forever trying to get engaged to whatever trollop he was going with at the time – a spoiled pup, I thought him.

I had never noticed before how lovingly and carefully the two sects were kept apart. That was probably why Winifred caused her parents more concern than Ernest did. She and Maire were both learning the piano from old Streichl, and they became great friends. The Dalys' was a great house in those days. Mick Daly was a builder; a tall, thin, sardonic man who, after long and bitter experience, had come to the conclusion that the whole town was in a conspiracy against him, and that his family – all but his wife, whom he regarded as a friendly neutral – was allied with the town. His wife was a handsome woman, whose relations with the enemy were far closer than her husband ever suspected. As for the traitors – Joe, Maire, Brenda, and Peter, the baby – they had voices like trumpets from shouting one another down, and exceedingly dirty tongues to use when the vocal chords gave out.

Joe was the eldest. He was a lad with a great head for whiskey and an even better one for books, if only he had taken them seriously, but it was a convention of the Daly family not to take anything seriously but money and advancement. Like other conventions this was not always observed in practice, but in theory it was always accepted, except by Peter, who later became a Jesuit, and Peter was no advertisement for unconventionality, having something in common with a submarine. He was a handsome lad with an enormous brow and bright blue eyes, and when he was submerged had a tendency to cut you dead in the street. For weeks he sat in his room, reading with ferocity, and then suddenly decided to come up for air and a little light conversation, and argued like a mad dog with you until two in the morning. At the time I speak of he happened to be a roaring atheist, as a result of an overdose of St Thomas Aquinas, and described me to Joe as 'just another belly-thumping image-worshipper'. That, the Dalys said flatly, was what reading did for you.

Yet it was a wonderful house on a Sunday evening when the children and their friends were in, and old Daly concluded an armistice with them for the evening. There was always lashings of stuff, because the Dalys, for all their worldly wisdom, could do nothing in a small and niggardly way. If you asked one of them for a cigarette, you were quite liable to be given a box of a hundred, and attempting to repay it might well be regarded as a deadly insult. Brenda, the younger girl, slouched round with sandwiches and gibes; Joe sang 'Even Bravest Heart May Swell' with an adoring leer at Maire, who played his accompaniment, when he came to 'Loving smile of sister kind', and Maire said furiously: 'Of all the bloody nonsense! A puck in the gob was all we ever got.'

'Really, they are an extraordinary family,' Winifred said with a sigh as I saw her home one night.

I didn't take it as criticism. Having been brought up in a fairly quiet home myself, I sometimes felt the same bewilderment.

'Isn't that what you like about them?' I asked.

'Is it, do you think?' she asked in surprise. 'I dare say you're right. I only wish Daddy thought the same.'

'What does he object to?' I asked.

'Oh, nothing in particular,' she replied with a shrug. ' "Just the wrong persuasion, dear." Haven't I nice girls of my own sort to mix with? Don't I realize that everything said in that house is reported in confession? . . . By the way, Dan, is it?'

'Not everything.'

'I hardly thought so,' she said dryly. 'Anyhow, they can confess anything I say to them.'

'You're not afraid of being converted?' I asked.

'Oh, anybody is welcome to try,' she said indifferently. 'Really, people are absurd about religion.'

I didn't say that some such ambition wasn't very far from Mrs Daly's mind. I had seen for myself that she liked Winifred and thought her good company for Maire, who was a bit on the wild side, and it was only natural that a woman so big-hearted should feel it a pity that a nice girl like Winifred dug with the wrong foot. It probably wasn't necessary to tell Winifred. There was little about the Dalys that she wasn't shrewd enough to observe for herself. That was part of *their* charm.

But, all the same, her parents had good ground for worry. What began as a friendship between herself and Maire continued as a love affair between herself and Joe. It came to a head during the summer holidays when the Dalys took a house in Crosshaven, and Winifred stayed with them. I went down for occasional weekends, and found it just like Cork, only worse. By some mysterious mental process, Mr

Daly had worked out that, as part of a general conspiracy, the property-owners in Crosshaven charged outrageous rents and then encouraged you to dissipate the benefits of your holiday by keeping you up all night, so he insisted on everyone's being in bed by eleven. With the connivance of the neutral power we all slipped out again when he was asleep for a dance in some neighbour's house, a moonlight swim or row, or walk along the cliffs. I was surprised at the change in Winifred. When I had first known her she was prim and demure, and when she was ragged about it, inclined to be truculent and awkward, but now she had grown to accept the ragging that was part of the Dalys' life and evolved a droll and impudent defence which gave the people the impression that it was she who was making fun of them. Irish Catholics don't like to be made fun of, so naturally this line was far more effective.

'She's coming on,' I said to Maire one evening when we were lying on the cliffs.

'She's getting more natural,' Maire admitted. 'At first she'd disgrace you. It wasn't bad enough wanting to pay for her own tea, but when she gave me the penny for the bus I thought I'd die of shame. I was so damn flabbergasted I took it from her.'

The picture of Maire taking a penny made me laugh outright, because she, too, had all the Daly lavishness, and there was nothing flashy or common about it. It was just that the story of their lives was written like that, in large capital letters.

'It's all damn well for you,' said Maire, who had no notion what I was laughing at. 'That damn family of hers must be as mean as hell.'

'Not mean,' I said. 'Just prudent.'

'Prudent!'

'Where is she now?'

'Being imprudent, I hope. Joe and herself are doing a terrible line. She'd be grand for him. She'd keep him in his place.'

'Why? Does he need to be kept in his place?' I asked.

'Joe? That fellow is as big a bully as Father,' said Maire,

busy tickling my nose with a blade of grass she had been chewing. 'God, the way Mother ruins that fellow! She'd order you out of the lavatory the way he wouldn't have to wait. Nobody is going to walk on Winifred. Aren't Protestants great, Dan?'

'We'll see when her family hears about herself and Joe,' I said.

'Oh, they're kicking up bloody murder about that already,' Maire said, throwing away one blade of grass and picking another to chew – a most restless woman! 'They think the Pope sicked him on to her.'

'And didn't he?'

'Is it Mother?' said Maire with a laugh. 'Would you blame her? Two birds with one stone – a wife for Joe and a soul for God! The poor woman would die happy.'

After that I watched Winifred's romance with real sympathy, perhaps with a reminiscence of *Romeo and Juliet* in my mind, perhaps already with a feeling of revolt against the cliques and factions of a provincial town. For a time it almost meant more to me than my own affair with Maire.

It didn't last though. One autumn evening when I was coming home from the office I saw Winifred emerge from a house on Summerhill. She saw me too and waved, and then came charging after me with her long legs flying. She always remained leggy and bird-like even in middle age; a tall, thin girl with a long, eager face, blue eyes and fair hair that wouldn't stay fixed. When she caught up on me she took my arm. That was the sort of thing I liked about her: the way she ran, the way she grabbed your arm, the way she burst into spontaneous intimacy with no calculation behind it.

'How's Joe?' I asked. 'I haven't seen him this past week.'

'No more have I, Dan,' she said lightly enough.

'How's that?' I asked gravely. 'I thought you'd be giving us a night by this time.'

'Ah, I don't think it'll ever come to that, Dan,' she replied in the same light-hearted tone, without any regret that I could detect.

'You're not going to disappoint us?' I asked, and I fancy

there must have been more feeling in my voice than in hers.

'Well, we've discussed it, of course,' she said in a business-like tone. 'But he can't marry me unless I become a Catholic.'

'Can't he?' I asked.

'Well, I suppose he couldn't be stopped if he took it into his head, but can you imagine Joe doing a daft thing like that? You know how it would affect his business.'

'I dare say it would,' I said, and mind you, it was the first time the idea of a thing like that had crossed my mind – I must have been more sentimental than I know, even now. 'But you could get a dispensation.'

'*If* I agreed to have the children brought up as Catholics.'

'Och, to hell with the children!' I said. 'They're all in the future. Why wouldn't you agree?'

'Really, Dan, how could I?' she asked wearily, giving my arm a tug. 'It's all that the parents threatened me with from the beginning. Oh dear! I suppose it was wrong of me to start anything at all with Joe, but no matter how fond of him I am, I can't walk out on them now.'

'It's your life, not theirs,' I said.

'Even so, Dan, I have to consider their feelings as Joe has to consider his parents' feelings. His mother wouldn't like to see her grandchildren brought up as Protestants, and my parents feel just the same. You may think they're wrong, but it would hurt them just as much as if they were right.'

'I think the sooner people with opinions like that get hurt, the better,' I said with a dull feeling of disappointment.

'Oh, I know!' she retorted, dropping my arm and flaring up at me like a real little termagant. 'I'm a Protestant, so I'm a freak, and it's up to me to make all the sacrifices.'

We were passing St Luke's Cross at the time, and I stopped dead and looked at her. Up to this I thought I'd never felt so intensely about anything. It didn't even occur to me that we were standing outside the church she worshipped in.

'If that's the sort you think I am, you're very much

mistaken,' I said. 'If you were my girl I wouldn't let God, man or devil come between us.'

Her face suddenly cleared and she grasped my arm.

'You know, Dan, I almost wish I was,' she said in a curious ringing tone.

Anyone who didn't know her would have taken that for an invitation, but even then, emotional as I was, I knew it was nothing of the sort. I think if I'd tried to slink inside Joe at that moment she'd have hated me for the rest of my life. Whatever it was she had to give was already given to Joe.

The following evening I went for a walk with Joe up the Western Road and we had it out. It was a queer conversation. I was at my worst, and Joe was at his best, and I remember his sensitiveness and my own awkwardness as if it was only yesterday.

'I had a talk with Winifred last night,' I said. 'I hope you won't think me interfering if I mention it to you.'

'I know anything you said would be kindly meant, Dan,' he said gently.

This was one of the many nice things about Joe. However much of a bully he might be, you did not have to skirmish for position with him. It had something to do with the capital letters that the Dalys used as if by nature.

'I think she's very fond of you, Joe,' I said.

'I think the same, Dan,' he agreed warmly. 'And 'tisn't all on one side. I needn't tell you that.'

'You couldn't come to some agreement with her about the religious business?' I asked.

'I'd like to know what agreement we could come to,' he said gravely. 'I can talk to you about it because you know what it means. You know what would happen to the business if I defied everybody and married Winifred in a register office.'

'But you want her to do it instead, Joe,' I said.

' 'Tisn't alike, Dan,' he said in his monumental way. 'And you know 'tisn't alike. It might have been different a hundred years ago – even fifty years ago. But this is a Catholic country now. Her people haven't the power they had, and they're not going to risk their own position bringing business to a lapsed Catholic. It might mean ruin to me, but it would mean nothing to Winifred.'

'That only makes it worse,' I said. 'You want her to give up a religion that she believes in for one that means nothing to you, only the harm it could do your business.'

'I never said it meant nothing to me,' he said with a smile. 'It means a lot, as a matter of fact. But you've shifted your ground, Dan. That's a different proposition entirely. We were talking about my responsibility to provide for a family.'

'Very well, then,' I said, thinking I saw a way out. 'Tell her that! Tell her what you've told me; that you'll marry her your way and take the responsibility, or marry her her way and let her take it.'

'Aren't you forgetting that a man can't shift the responsibility for a family, Dan?' he asked, laying a friendly hand on my shoulder.

'She can see that as well as I can, and she won't take the responsibility,' I said.

'Ah, well, Dan, she mightn't be as intelligent as you about it, and then I'd have to face the consequences just the same.'

'You won't have any consequences to face, Joe,' I said. 'She's not that sort of a girl at all.'

'Dan, I'm beginning to think you're the one who should marry her,' he said jokingly.

'I'm beginning to think the same,' I said, getting into a huff.

We dropped the subject, and we never discussed it again, but I'd still take my dying oath that if he'd done what I suggested she'd have pitched her family to blazes and married him. All a girl like that wanted was proof that he cared enough about her to take a risk, and after it she'd spend her life seeing that he didn't pay for it. Capital letters are not enough where love is concerned. You want something more. Nowadays I don't blame him, but at that age when you feel a friend must be everything from Solomon to Julius Caesar I felt hurt and disillusioned.

Winifred wasted no tears over him, and in a few months

was walking out in a practical way with a schoolteacher of her own persuasion – whoever persuaded them. She still called at the Dalys, but things were not the same. Mrs Daly was disappointed in her. It struck her as strange that an intelligent girl like Winifred could not see the errors of Protestantism for herself, and, from the moment she knew that there was to be no spectacular public conversion, gave her up as a bad job. She told me that she had never approved of mixed marriages, and for once she got me really angry.

'All marriages are mixed marriages, Mrs Daly,' I said stiffly. 'They're all right when the mixture is all right.'

It was about that time that I began to notice that the mixture of Maire and myself wasn't all right. It was partly the feeling that the house was not the same without Winifred there. She hadn't been there when I knew the Dalys first, but that made no difference. These things happen to people and places: some light goes out in them, and afterwards they are never the same again. Maire said the change was in me, and that I was becoming conceited and irritable. Maybe she was right.

But for months I was sore about it. It wasn't Maire I missed so much as the family. My own home life had been too quiet, and I had loved the capital letters, the gaiety and the tantrums. I had now drifted into another spell of loneliness, but loneliness with a new and disturbing feeling of alienation; and Cork is a bad place for a man who feels like that. It was as if I couldn't communicate with anybody. On Sundays, instead of going to Mass, I walked down the quays and along the river. It was pleasant there, and I sat on a bench under the trees and watched the reflection of the big painted houses and the cliffs behind them in the water, or read some book. A long, leisurely book – it looked as though I should have a lifetime to read it in.

I had been doing it for months when, one day, I noticed a man who turned up each Sunday about the same time. I knew him; he was a teacher from the South Side. We chatted, and the following Sunday when we met again he said quizzically:

'You seem to be very fond of ships.'

'Mr Reilly,' I said, 'those that go down to the sea in ships are to me the greatest wonder of the Lord.'

'Oh, is that so?' he said without surprise. 'I just wondered when I saw you here so much.'

That morning I was feeling depressed and resentful, and I didn't care much whom I told about it.

'It happens to be the most convenient quiet spot to the church where my family think I am at the moment,' I said.

'I fancied that from the book you have under your arm,' he said with amusement. 'I wouldn't let too many people see that book if I was you. They might misunderstand you.' Then, noticing a third man we had both seen before, he added: 'I wonder would he by any chance be doing the same thing.'

As a matter of fact he was. It was remarkable, after we got to know one another, the number of educated men who found their way to the Marina Walk on Sunday mornings. Reilly called us 'The Atheists' Club', but that was only swank because we had only one atheist. Reilly and myself were mild agnostics, and the rest were anti-clericals or young fellows with doubts. All this revealed itself very gradually in our Sunday morning talks. It was also revealed to me that I wasn't the only young man in town who was lonely and dissatisfied.

After Winifred got married I visited her a couple of times, and her husband and I got on well together. He was a plump, jolly, good-natured man, fond of his game of golf and his glass of whiskey, and I had the impression that Winifred and himself hit it off excellently. They had two sons. Joe never gave her any great cause to regret him because, though his business prospered, he proved a handful for the girl who got him. Drink was his trouble, and he bore it with great dignity. At one time half the police in Cork seemed to be exclusively engaged in getting him home to prevent his being charged with drunkenness and disorderly conduct by the other half, and except for one small fine for being on unlicensed premises after hours – a young policeman was responsible for that and he was transferred immediately – he never was charged.

But, of course, we all drifted apart. Ten years later, when I read that Winifred's husband was dead, I went to the funeral for the sake of old times, saw nobody I knew there and slipped away again before it reached the cemetery.

A couple of months later, I strolled back from the Atheists' Club one Sunday morning as Mass was ending to pick up two orthodox acquaintances who I knew would be at it. It was a sunny day: the church, as usual, was crammed, and I stood on the pavement, watching the crowds pour down the steps and thinking how much out of it all I was. Suddenly I caught a glimpse of Winifred passing under the portico at right angles in the direction of the back gate. She had the two children with her, and it was only the sight of these that convinced me I wasn't imagining it. I dashed through the crowd to reach her, and the moment she saw me her face lit up. She caught my hands – it was one of those instinctive gestures that at once brought back old times to me.

'Dan!' she cried in astonishment. 'What on earth brings you here?'

'Young lady,' I said, 'I am *not* here, and anyway I'm the one that should ask that question.'

'Oh, it's a long story,' she said with a laugh. 'If you're coming back my way I might tell you, and I'm sure there's a bottle of stout at home ... Run along, Willie!' she sang out to the elder boy, and he and his brother went ahead of us up the steps.

'I wouldn't have believed it of you,' I said.

'Ah, what is there to keep me back now?' she said with a shrug. 'Daddy and Mummy are dead, and you know how much Ernest cares what I do.'

'Well, you still seem quite cheerful,' I said. 'Almost as cheerful as a roaring agnostic like myself.'

'Ah, but look at you, Dan!' she said mockingly, taking my hand again without the least trace of self-consciousness. 'A bachelor, with nothing in the world to worry about! Why on earth wouldn't you be cheerful?'

I nearly told her why but thought better of it. It was too like her own story, but her way out could never be mine. Besides, if I decided now to try to get on the same terms with her as I had once almost done from blind rage, the position would be reversed. It was I and not she who would have to sign on the dotted line. But for the first time I understood how her life had gone awry. A woman always tries to give the children she loves whatever it is she feels she has missed in life. Often you don't even know what it was till you see what it is she is trying to give them. Perhaps she doesn't know herself. With some it's money, with others it's education; with others still, it is just love. And the kids never value it, of course. How could they when they've never known the lack of it?

And there, as we sat over our drinks in the front room of her little house, two old cronies, I thought how strange it was that the same thing had sent us in opposite directions. A man and a woman in search of something are always driven apart, but it is the same thing that drives them.

Travellers' Samples (1951)

THIS MORTAL COIL

Every Sunday morning, at a time when the rest of the city was at church, a few of us met on the river bank. We were the people who didn't believe in church, and we ranged from a seminarist with scruples to a roaring atheist. It was curious, the discussions and confessions you heard there. I often thought it must have been like that in the early days of Christianity. Youth, of course, will turn anything into a religion – even having no religion at all.

Curious friendships sprang up as well, like the one between me and Dan Turner. Dan was our atheist, and the one I liked best. He was a well-built, fresh-coloured man who looked like a sailor or a farmer, but he was really a County Council clerk. Part of my sympathy for him was because of the way he was penalized for his opinions. Long before, at the age of eighteen, he had had to give evidence in a taxation case and insisted on making a declaration instead of taking the oath. That finished him. Though he was easily the cleverest man in the Courthouse, he would never be secretary or anything approaching it. And knowing this, and knowing all the intrigues that went on against him, only made him more positive and truculent.

Not that he thought of himself as either; in his own opinion he was a perfect example of the English genius for compromise, but the nearest he ever got to ignoring some remark he disagreed with was to raise his eyebrows into his hair, turn his blue eyes the other way, and whistle. A man who might be inclined to overlook a spot of atheism would not overlook a whistle.

'Och, Dan, you take things to the fair,' I said to him once.

'All I ask is that bloody idiots will keep their opinions to themselves and not be airing them on me,' he said in the tone of a reasonable man who was only asking that people shouldn't spit on the dining-room carpet.

'If you want people to behave like that, you should go somewhere you won't be a target for them,' I said.

'And if we all did that, this country would never be anything only a home for idiots,' he said saucily.

'Oh, if you only want to make a martyr of yourself in the interests of the country, that's different,' I said. 'But it seems to me very queer conduct for a man who calls himself a rationalist. I call that sentimentality.'

He nearly struck me for calling it sentimentality, but of course, that's what it was, really. If you ask me, that's what atheism is – sentimental agnosticism. And, for all Dan's brains, he was as emotional as a child. He was cut to the heart by the intrigues against him. He lived in an old house on the quays with a pious old maid sister called Madge who adored him, cluck-clucked and tut-tutted his most extravagant statements and went to Mass every morning to pray for his conversion. He didn't like it, but he knew that she would never marry and that he would have to support her till the day she died, and he was too big a man to emphasize her dependence on him. It was only when she really drove him insane telling him about miraculous apparitions in Donegal that he blew up on her.

'That's not religion at all, woman,' he would shout, slapping the arm of his chair in vexation. 'That's only barbarous superstition.' But Madge only pitied and loved him the more for it, and went on in her own way believing in God, ghosts, fairies, and nutmegs for lumbago.

It wasn't until well into his thirties that Dan fell in love, and then he did it in a way that no rationalist could approve of. Tessa Bridie wasn't very young either, but, like many another fine girl in the provinces, she found that the fellows who wanted to marry her were not always those she wanted to marry. Also, like many another fine girl, she was holding on like grim death to a clerk in an insurance office called MacGuinness, with jet-black curly hair, nationalist sentiments and great aspirations after the religious life, which, I suppose, is the only sort of life a clerk in an insurance office can aspire to.

Dan and Tessa made a nice pair. They both had plenty of character and intelligence, and in a town like ours meeting someone you can fall in love with and at the same time talk intelligently to is a thing you dream about. But the damn atheistic nonsense would keep cropping up. Tessa was convinced for a long time that Dan was the answer to her prayers, but Dan in his simple, straightforward way wouldn't let her be. He had to prove to her that he couldn't be the answer to anyone's prayer, because there was nobody to answer prayers, and it was foolishness – foolishness and worse – to imagine that they could be answered.

Now, Tessa wasn't by any means a bigoted girl: she had several brothers, and she knew that in the matter of religion and politics every man without exception had a slate loose somewhere, but Dan was out on his own. She started a novena for enlightenment, hoping to bring in a verdict in his favour, but she was so acutely aware that he thought there was no enlightenment either that the novena came out the wrong way. With his English tendency to compromise, Dan cursed and swore; assured her that he was the most tolerant man in the bloody world, and that she could believe in any damn childish nonsense she liked so long as she married him, but Dan's compromise frightened her more than another man's intransigence and she got engaged to the insurance man. I thought it a pity, because she was a really nice intelligent girl, and I was sure that a couple of kids would lower Dan's voltage quite a bit.

What the other thing would do to him I didn't know but I soon found out. It seemed he had deserted all his old haunts (he no longer came down the river on Sundays), was off eating and talking, and didn't stir out at night until after dark, when he went for long, lonesome walks in the country. People who had met him talked about the way he passed them without recognition or with a curt nod. I knew the symptoms. I knew them only too well, and I felt it was up to me to do something. One fine evening I called. Madge opened the door, and I could see she had been crying.

'I didn't see Dan this long time, Madge,' I said. 'How is he?'

'Come in, Michael John,' she said, taking out her handkerchief. 'He's upstairs. He didn't stir out this past couple of days. Sure, you know the County Council will never stand it.'

I followed her up the stairs. Dan was lying on his bed, dressed except for a collar and tie, his two hands under his head, apparently studying the ceiling and finding it very unsatisfactory. When I came in he raised his brows with his usual look of blank astonishment as much as to say: 'Can't I have even a moment's peace in this house?'

'Would you like a cup of tea, Dan?' Madge asked anxiously.

'If it's for me you needn't mind,' said Dan with a patient long-suffering air that made it plain what he thought of the suggestion that he could be snatched back from the gates of the grave by a cup of tea.

'Wisha, I'm sure Michael John would like one,' Madge said in a wail.

'You're not feeling well, I hear?' I said.

'I don't know how you heard anything of the kind,' said

Dan, rolling his blue eyes to the other side of the room. 'I'm sure I didn't complain.'

'Wisha, Michael John,' Madge burst out, 'did you ever in all your life hear of a grown man carrying on like that on account of a woman?'

'Now, I told you before I wasn't going to discuss my business with you,' Dan said, raising the palm of his hand between them like a partition wall.

'Why then, indeed, she discussed it enough with everybody,' Madge said, not realizing how every word hurt. 'There wasn't much about you that she didn't repeat. How well I could hear it all from a woman in the market!'

'Well, go back and discuss it with the woman in the market,' he retorted brutally. She gave me a tearful smile and went downstairs.

'You have a grand view,' I said, looking down on the quays and the three-master below the bridge in the dusk.

'There isn't the traffic there used to be,' he said grudgingly.

'You never wanted to be a sailor?' I asked.

'I was never asked,' he replied, as if this were one grievance he hadn't thought of. 'No one ever consulted me about what I wanted to be.'

I looked again at the shelf of books by the bed; a few popular books on physics and a fine collection of history and historical memoirs. History is a grand source for unbelievers.

'What you need is a holiday,' I said.

'How can I take a holiday?' he asked, turning his blue eyes wonderingly on me as if he had discovered that I was only another of his persecutors.

'If you go on like this you'll take a holiday whether you like it or not,' I said. 'And it won't be by the seaside either. What about Ballybunion for a week?'

The eyebrows went up again.

'Parish priests.'

'All right,' I said. 'We'll go where there are no parish priests.'

'We'll travel a hell of a distance,' he said despondently, but all the same the idea appealed to him. 'I'd like to see London again. 'Tis ten years since I was there last.'

It almost put him into a good humour, and when I was leaving he put on a collar and tie and walked home with me. I could see that Madge was well-pleased, and I wasn't too dissatisfied myself.

But the pleasure didn't last long. Next morning I was at work when she called for me. She could scarcely speak for terror.

'Michael John, something awful is after happening,' she said. ' 'Tis Dan. I don't know what to do with him. He tried to commit suicide.'

'He what?' I said.

'He did, Michael John. After he came home last night. He turned on the gas tap before he went to bed. I know because I could still smell it this morning. He's in bed now with a roaring headache.' Then she began to cry. 'Sure, anyone could have told him you couldn't commit suicide with the gas we have in our house.'

I told her I'd be down that night and try to get him away by Saturday. It was all I could think of. Suicide was a thing I had no experience of because in our class a man's family and friends would never let him go so far. It was only when a man or woman had nobody that they were found in the river, and then it was always brought in as accidental death not to depress the neighbours.

I didn't know what the best thing was, so I bought a bottle of whiskey and a few gramophone records. Whenever I feel like committing suicide myself I usually go out and buy something extravagant because after such a tribute of respect to myself I feel less like depriving the community of my services.

Dan was sitting in the front room when I went in, still without a collar and tie, and he barely lifted his eyes to salute me. With the dusk coming down on the river outside, he seemed so lonesome, so shut away in his own doubt and gloom, that he almost reduced me to the same state. Believe me, you can be very lonely in a provincial town.

'Well, I got leave from Saturday if you're ready to start,' I said, trying to make my voice sound as much like a hunting horn as possible.

'I don't know that I'll be able,' he replied in a dead voice, as though the words were merely a momentary interruption of a train of thought that was too strong for him.

'You'll have to,' I said. 'You can't go on like this much longer.'

'I wasn't thinking of going on much longer,' he said in the same tone.

'Why?' I asked, raising my voice and trying to make a joke of it. 'You weren't thinking of chucking yourself in the river or anything?'

'I suppose a man might as well do that as anything else.'

'Ah, look here, Dan,' I said, opening the bottle of whiskey, 'we all think like that at times, and it's only a mug's game. In a week's time you'll be laughing at it.'

'Of course, if you're not there in a week's time, you won't have an opportunity of laughing at it.'

'That's why it's a mug's game,' I said, filling him out a stiff drink. 'Doing something permanent about something temporary is always a mug's game.'

'Life itself is a pretty temporary affair, I always understood,' he said.

'It goes on quite a while, just the same,' said I. 'How old are you? Thirty-five?'

'Thirty-eight,' he said in the tone of an old paralytic telling you he's eighty-three and will be glad when the Lord takes him. 'And what has a man of thirty-eight to look forward to in this country?'

'Being thirty-nine,' said I.

'It's hardly likely to be much pleasanter than being thirty-eight,' he said. 'And that, let me tell you, is no great shakes.'

I sat opposite him with my whiskey, while he continued to look at me moodily, a big, powerful, red-faced man, his hands over the arms of his chair, his head lowered, his eyebrows raised, the blue smouldering eyes in ambush beneath them.

'The trouble with you, Dan, is that you're under two illusions,' I said. 'One is that everyone except yourself is having a lovely time; the other is that when you're dead, your troubles are over.'

That roused him all right.

'That's not an illusion,' he said, raising his voice. 'That's a scientific fact.'

'Fact, my nanny!' I said. 'How do you know?'

' 'Tis a fact that anyone can see with his own two eyes,' he said, getting angrier and more positive.

'Well, I can't see it for one,' I said.

'You can see it, but you don't want to see it,' he said, tossing his big head as though he was going to gore me. 'It doesn't suit you to see it. You're like all the other optimistic gentlemen who pretend they can't see it. My God!' he said, beginning to splutter with rage. 'The vanity and conceit of people imagining that their own miserable little existence is too valuable to be wiped out!'

Then I began to get angry too. Forgetting he was a sick man, I wanted to take it out on him for his unmannerly arrogance and complacency.

'And who the hell are you?' I asked. 'Who told you you were alive in the first place?'

'Who told me?' he repeated, a bit shaken. 'No one told me. I am alive. If I didn't know that I wouldn't know anything.'

'And what *do* you know?' I shouted. 'As long as you can't tell me who you really are, or what you're doing in this room at this moment, you have no right to tell me in that impudent tone that you know what's going to happen to you when you die.'

He considered that for a moment. I fancy it had never occurred to him in his life before that a man of his strong character mightn't be as real as he thought himself and that he didn't quite know how to answer me.

'I admit there are things you can't explain yet,' he said grudgingly.

'Nor ever will be able to explain,' I said.

'Everything can be explained,' he said, getting mad again.

'Not things that are deliberately intended not to be explained,' said I.

'Oh, so you think it's all deliberate?' he said mocking me.

'If you think at all, you have to think that,' said I. 'You can no more live without doubt than you can live without air – doubt about what's going to happen tomorrow, doubt about what's going to happen next year, doubt about a future life.'

'Plenty of people think they know all about the future life.'

'They have faith,' I said. 'But you can't have faith unless you have doubt.'

'They have more than faith, Mr O'D,' he said saucily. 'According to themselves they have actual knowledge.'

'More than faith is no faith at all,' said I. 'They're just like you, pretending to know. Damn it, doubt is the first principle of existence, and ye go round trying to destroy it in other people. If you knew what you let on to know, you wouldn't be planning to go to England on Saturday.'

'I'm not so sure that I'm going to England on Saturday,' he said, getting despondent again.

But the argument did him good; it gave him something to think about. The only mistake I made was in thinking that a man as headstrong as that could ever be impressed for long by an argument. We went on to some music; Madge came into the room to listen, and it was quite like old times. He saw me off at the door. It was a lovely starlit night, and he leaned against the door jamb, talking and cocking his head at the voices of girls and sailors from way down the river.

Next morning, I was barely into work before a couple of the men came up to tell me about the fellow who had been fished out of the river that morning. My heart sank. I didn't need anyone to tell me who it was.

I left word that I probably wouldn't be back and set off down the quays. They were very quiet, and the church and the trees were reflected in the water, almost without a ripple. I was blaming myself terribly for the whole business, though I still didn't see what I could have done. There were a couple of women standing outside the house, gossiping, and there was a trail of water from the quayside to the hall door.

Madge opened the door and put her finger hastily to her lips. I couldn't understand it. She didn't look in the least con-cerned. She beckoned me up the stairs, and pointed to the wet trail on the carpet. There was a shocking smell of gas.

She opened the door of Dan's room, and when we went in, closed it behind us. The window was wide open; the bed had not been slept in, and there was a tea-chest in the middle of the floor.

'What did they do with him, Madge?' I whispered.

'Dan?' she said in surprise. 'Oh, he's downstairs, at his breakfast, I only wanted you to see for yourself. Otherwise you mightn't believe it.'

'You mean they got him out all right?' I asked.

'It was the mercy of God the sailor saw him,' she said with shining eyes. 'He couldn't swim with his boots on.'

'But how the hell did he do it?' I asked.

'Don't you see?' she said, pointing to the tea-chest. 'He had a length of tubing running into this, with a tap on it.'

She raised the tea-chest so that I could see the hole drilled in the side. Beneath it was a pillow and a rug.

'But what's it for?' I asked.

'He bought the tubing and the tap so that he could turn on the gas when he was inside the tea-chest,' said Madge with a smile. 'The notion of him being kept down by a tea-chest, that two men couldn't control when he had the pneumonia! He must have been lifting it off him the whole time. You can see where he got sick through the window.'

'And after going through that jigmareel, he went and threw himself in the river!' I said, marvelling at the stubbornness of the man.

'Ah, that was this morning, Michael John,' said Madge ingenuously. 'Before that, he saw a great light.'

'A great what?' I asked.

'A great light,' said Madge. 'He saw that life was good after all.'

'He saw a hell of a lot,' I said sourly.

'He said suddenly the whole thing became plain to him,' said Madge. 'So to put temptation away from him, he took the tube and the tap to throw them in the river. It was while he was doing that he tripped over the rope.'

'I see,' I said nastily. 'He saw the light, but he didn't see the rope.'

Her eyes filled with tears.

'Don't be hard on him, Michael John,' she said, shaking her head. 'He got a terrible fright, the poor creature. When they brought him in he was sobbing and shaking like a little child. "I thought 'twas goodbye, Madge," he said. Whatever you do, don't upset him again on me. He's the best brother in the world only for the misfortunate books he reads. 'Tis them I'd like to throw in the river.'

She gave a heart-scalded look at the shelf of books by Dan's bed.

I went downstairs in a sort of stupor, not knowing what I was to think or say. Naturally, I didn't believe in the accident. I was only wondering what plan Dan would try next and how I'd stop him. He was sitting in the kitchen in his best suit, finishing his breakfast and reading the morning paper – a nice domestic spectacle after a performance like that.

'Oughtn't you to be damn well ashamed of yourself?' I said, losing all control at the sight of him.

'Ashamed of myself?' he asked sarcastically, raising his big brows in the old supercilious way. 'I don't see any particular reason for being ashamed of myself. I suppose an accident can happen to anyone?'

'Accident!' I said. 'And wasn't I sitting in this house with you last night, trying to keep you from any more accidents? What sort of way is this to treat your unfortunate sister?'

Suddenly a strange look came over his face. He bowed his head and nodded.

'I admit that,' he said meekly. 'I admit I was headstrong.'

'Headstrong, and inconsiderate, and conceited, and imagining you were the only one in the world who knew anything.'

'I know, I know,' he said. 'I was a terrible egotist. There's a lot of things I have to change in my character.'

At that I didn't know what to say. Dan Turner admitting that there were things in his character he had to change! It was an accident all right.

Of course, Madge wouldn't admit that. She was convinced it was a miracle. It made a different man of Dan, and the funny thing is nowadays he'd squeeze through a keyhole to

155

get away from me. He says I'm a dangerous influence; a man of no conviction. Because now he knows precisely what's waiting for him when he dies, only that it happens to be quite different from what he knew was waiting for him before.

And, of course, I just go on doubting.

THE SENTRY

Father MacEnerney was finding it hard to keep Sister Margaret from exploding. The woman was lonesome, but he was lonesome himself. He liked his little parish outside the big military camp near Salisbury; he liked the country and the people, and he liked his little garden, even if it was raided twice a week by the soldiers. But he did suffer from lack of friends. Apart from his housekeeper and a couple of private soldiers in the camp, the only Irish people he could talk to were the three Irish nuns in the convent, and that was why he went there so often for his supper and to say his office in the convent garden.

Even here his peace was now being threatened by Sister Margaret's obstreperousness. Of course, the trouble was that before the war fathers, mothers, sisters and brothers as well as odd aunts and cousins had looked into the convent or spent a few days at the inn; and every week, long, juicy letters had arrived from home, telling the nuns by what political intrigue Paddy Dunphy had had himself appointed warble-fly inspector for the Benlicky area; but now it was years since anyone from Ireland had called, and the letters from home were censored at both sides of the channel by inquisitive girls with a taste for scandal till a sort of creeping paralysis seized up every form of intimacy. Sister Margaret was the worst hit, because a girl from her own town was in the Dublin censorship, and, according to Sister Margaret, she was a scandalmonger of the most objectionable kind. Naturally, she took it out on the English nuns.

'Oh, Father Michael,' she sighed one evening when they were walking round the garden, 'I'm afraid I made a great mistake. A terrible mistake! I don't know how it is, but the English seem to me to have no nature.'

'Ah, I wouldn't say that,' protested Father MacEnerney in his deep, sombre voice. 'They have their little ways, and we have ours, and if we both knew more about one another we'd get on better.'

To illustrate what he meant, he told her about old Father Dan Murphy, a Tipperary priest who had spent his life on the Mission, and the English Bishop. The Bishop was a decent, honourable little man, but quite unable to understand the feelings of his Irish priests. One evening Father Dan had called on Father MacEnerney. He was in a terrible state. He had received a terrible letter from the Bishop. It was so terrible he couldn't even show it. He would just have to go home. No, it wasn't so much anything the Bishop had said as the way he had said it. Finally, when Father MacEnerney had pressed him hard enough, he broke down and whispered that the Bishop had begun his letter with 'Dear Murphy'. 'As if he was writing to a farmhand, father.'

Father MacEnerney laughed, but it was no laughing matter to Sister Margaret. She clapped her hand to her mouth and stood looking at him.

'He didn't, Father Michael?' she said in an outraged tone.

So, seeing she didn't understand any better than Father Dan had, Father MacEnerney explained again that this was only how an Englishman would address anyone except a particular friend. A convention, nothing more.

'Ah, you're too simple, Father Michael,' Sister Margaret said indignantly. 'Convention, how are you? "Dear Murphy?" I'm surprised at you! What way is that to write to a priest? And how can they expect their own people to have any respect for religion when they have no respect for it themselves? Oh, that's the English all out! They try to domineer and bully you. Don't I have it every day of my life from them? "Dear Murphy"! I don't know how anybody can stand them.'

Sister Margaret was his best friend in the community: he knew that the other nuns relied on him to handle her for them, and it was a genuine worry to him to see her getting into this morbid state.

'Oh, come, come!' he said reproachfully. 'How well Sister Teresa and Sister Bonaventura can get on with them.'

'I suppose I shouldn't say it,' she said in a low, brooding voice. 'God forgive me, I can't help it. I'm afraid Sister Teresa and Sister Bonaventura are not *genuine*.'

'Now, you're not being fair,' he said gravely.

'And why should I be fair?' she cried. 'They're not genuine, and you know yourself they're not genuine. They're lick-spittles, father, lickspittles! They suck up to the English nuns the whole time. They take every sort of gibe and impertinence from them. They simply have no independence. You wouldn't believe it.'

'We all have to accept a lot for the sake of charity,' he said.

'I don't call that charity at all, father,' she replied, obstinately, and her big Kerry jaw stuck out. 'I call that moral cowardice. Why should the English have it all their own way? Even in religion they go on as if they owned the earth. They tell me I'm disloyal and a pro-German, and I ask them: "What did you ever do to make me anything else?" And then, they pretend that we were savages, and they came over and civilized us! Did you ever in all your life hear such impudence? People that were painting themselves all over when we were the Island of Saints and Scholars!'

'Well, of course that's all true enough but we must remember what they're going through,' he said.

'And what did we have to go through?' she asked shortly. 'Oh, now, father, it's all very well to be talking, but I don't see why we should have to make all the sacrifices. Why don't they think of all the terrible things they did to us? And all because we were true to our religion when they weren't! I'm after sending home for an Irish history, father, and mark my words, the next time one of them begins picking on me, I'll give her the answer. The impudence!'

Suddenly Father MacEnerney stopped and frowned.

'What is it, father?' she asked anxiously.

'Just a queer feeling I got,' he muttered. 'I was wondering was there someone at my onions.'

The sudden sensation was quite genuine, though it might have happened in a perfectly normal way, for his onions were the great anxiety of Father MacEnerney's life. He could grow them when the convent gardener couldn't, but, unlike the convent gardener, he had no way of guarding them. His housekeeper was elderly and frightened and pretended not to see what went on for fear the soldiers would take a fancy to her as well.

'They only wait till they get me out of their sight,' he said, and then got down and laid his ear to the earth. As a country boy he knew that the earth is a great conductor of sound.

'I was right,' he shouted triumphantly as he sprang to his feet and rushed for his bicycle. 'If I catch them at it they'll leave me alone for the future. I'll ring you up, Sister.'

A moment later, doubled over the handlebars, he was pedalling down the hill towards his house. As he passed the camp gate he noticed that there was no sentry on duty and knew he had one of the thieves at last. With a whoop of rage he threw his bicycle down by the gate and rushed across the garden. The sentry, a small man with fair hair, blue eyes and a worried expression, dropped the handful of onions he was holding. His rifle was standing by the wall.

'Aha, so I caught you at it!' shouted Father MacEnerney. He grabbed the sentry by the arm and twisted it viciously behind his back. 'So you're the fellow that was at my onions! Now you can come up to the camp with me and explain yourself.'

'I'm going, I'm going,' the sentry said in alarm, trying to wrench himself free.

'Oh, you're going all right,' the priest said, urging him forward with his knee. 'And I'm going with you.'

'Here, you let go of me!' the sentry cried. 'I haven't done anything, have I?'

'You haven't done anything!' the priest repeated bitterly. 'You weren't stealing my onions!'

'Don't you twist my wrist!' screamed the sentry, swinging round on him. 'Try to behave like a civilized human being. I didn't take your onions. I don't even know what you're talking about.'

'You dirty little English liar!' shouted Father MacEnerney, beside himself with rage at the impudence of the man. He dropped the sentry's wrist and pointed at the onions. 'Hadn't you them there in your hand, when I caught you? Didn't I see them with you, God blast you!'

'Oh, those things?' the sentry exclaimed as though he had suddenly seen a great light. 'Some kids dropped them and I picked them up.'

'You picked them up!' repeated Father MacEnerney sarcastically, drawing back his fist and making the sentry duck. 'You didn't even know they were onions, I suppose?'

'I didn't have much time to look, did I?' the sentry asked hysterically. 'I seen some kids in your garden, pulling the bleeding things. I told them get out and they only laughed at me. Then I chased them and they dropped these. What do you mean, twisting my wrist like that? I was only trying to do you a good turn. I've a good mind to give you in charge.'

The impudence was too much for the priest, who could not have thought up a yarn like that inside an hour. He never had liked liars anyway.

'You what?' he shouted, tearing off his coat. 'You'd give me in charge? I'd take ten little brats like you and break you across my knee. You bloody little English thief, take off your tunic!'

'I can't,' the sentry said in panic.

'Why can't you?'

'Because I'm on duty. You know that.'

'On duty! You're afraid.'

'I'm not afraid. I'll meet you anywhere you like, any time you like, and put your buck teeth through your fat head.'

'Then take off your tunic now and fight like a man.' He gave the sentry a punch that sent him staggering against the wall. 'Now will you fight, you dirty little English coward?'

'You know I can't fight,' panted the sentry, putting his arms up to protect himself. 'If I wasn't on duty I'd soon show you whether I'm a coward or not. You're the coward, not me, you dirty Irish bully! You know I'm on duty. You know I'm not in a position to protect myself. You're mighty cocky, just because you're in a privileged position, you mean, bullying bastard!'

Something in the sentry's tone halted the priest. He was almost hysterical. Father MacEnerney could not hit him while he was in that state.

'Get out of this so, God blast you!' he said furiously.

The sentry gave him a murderous look, then took up his rifle and walked back up the road to the camp gate. Father MacEnerney stared after him. He was furious. He wanted a fight, and if only the sentry had hit back would certainly have smashed him up. All the MacEnerneys were like that. His father was the quietest man in County Clare, but if you gave him occasion he would fight in a bag, tied up.

The priest went in to his own front room but found himself too upset to settle down. He sat in his big leather chair, trembling all over with suppressed violence. 'I'm too soft,' he thought despairingly. 'Too soft. It was my one opportunity and I didn't take advantage of it. Now they'll all know they can do what they like with me. I might as well give up trying to keep a garden. I might as well go back to Ireland. This is no country for anyone.' At last he went to the telephone and rang up Sister Margaret. Her voice, when she answered, was trembling with eagerness.

'Oh, father, did you catch them?' she cried.

'Yes,' he replied in an expressionless voice. 'I caught one of them anyway. A sentry.'

'And what did you do?'

'Gave him a clout,' he replied in the same tone.

'Oh, if 'twas me I'd have killed him,' she cried piteously.

'I'd have done that too, only he wouldn't fight,' Father

MacEnerney said gloomily. 'If I'm shot from behind a hedge one of these days you'll know who did it.'

'Oh, isn't that the English all out?' she said with hysterical disgust. 'They have so much old talk about their bravery, and when anyone stands up to them, they won't fight.'

'That's right,' he said, meaning it was wrong, and rang off. He realized that for once he and Sister Margaret were thinking alike, and that Sister Margaret was not right in the head. Suddenly his conduct appeared to him in its true light. He had behaved abominably. After all his talk of charity, he had insulted another man about his nationality, had hit him when he couldn't hit back, and only for that might have done him some serious injury – and all for a handful of onions worth sixpence! There was nice behaviour for a priest! There was good example for non-Catholics! He wondered what the Bishop would say if he heard that.

He sat back again in his chair, humped in dejection. His atrocious temper had betrayed him again. One of these days he knew it would land him in really serious trouble. And there were no amends he could make. He couldn't even go into the camp and apologize to the man without getting him into fresh trouble. He faithfully promised himself to apologize if he met him again.

This eased his conscience a little, and after saying Mass next morning he didn't feel quite so bad. The run across the downs in the early morning always gave him pleasure, and the view of the red-brick village with the white spire in a stagnant pool of dark trees below him. The barrows of old Celts showed on the polished surface of the chalk-green hills. They, poor devils, had had trouble with the English too, and got the worst of it.

He was nearly in good humour again when Elsie, the housekeeper, told him that there was an officer from the camp to see him. His guilty conscience started up again like an aching tooth. What the hell was it now?

The officer was a tall, good-looking young man with an obstinate jaw that stuck out like an advertisement for a shaving soap. He had a pleasant, jerky, friendly manner.

'Good morning, padre,' he said in a harsh voice. 'My name is Howe. I called about your garden. I believe our chaps have been giving you trouble.'

By this time Father MacEnerney would cheerfully have made him a present of the garden, onions and all.

'Ah, wasn't it my own fault for putting temptation in their way?' he asked with a sunny smile.

'Well, it's very nice of you to take it like that,' said the officer in a tone of mild surprise. 'The CO is rather indignant about it. He suggested barbed wire.'

'Electrified?' Father MacEnerney asked ironically.

'No, ordinary barbed wire,' Howe said, missing the joke completely. 'Pretty effective, you know.'

'Useless,' Father MacEnerney said promptly. 'Don't worry your head about it. You'll have a drop of Irish? And ice in it. Ah, go on, you will!'

'A bit early for me, I'm afraid,' Howe said with a glance at his watch.

'Coffee, so,' Father MacEnerney said authoritatively. 'No one leaves this house without some nourishment.'

He shouted to Elsie for more coffee and handed Howe a cigarette. Howe knocked it briskly on the chair and lit it.

'Now, this chap you caught last night – how much damage had he actually done?' he asked in a businesslike tone.

The question put Father MacEnerney more than ever on his guard. He wondered how the officer knew about it all.

'Which chap was this?' he asked, fighting a delaying action.

'The chap you beat up.'

'That I beat up,' echoed Father MacEnerney, aghast. 'Who said I beat him up?'

'He did. He expected you to report him, so he decided to give himself up. You seem to have scared him pretty badly.'

However Father MacEnerney might have scared the sentry, the sentry had now scared him worse. It seemed the thing was anything but over; if he wasn't careful, he might find himself involved as a witness against the sentry, and then the whole sordid story of his behaviour would emerge. It was just like the English to expect people to report them.

They took every damn thing literally, from a joke about electrified barbed wire to a fit of bad temper.

'But why would he expect me to report him?' he asked in confusion. 'When do you say this happened? Last night?'

'So I'm told,' Howe said shortly. He waited for Father MacEnerney to speak, and when he didn't, raised his voice as though he thought the priest might be deaf, or stupid, or both. 'I mean Collins, the man you caught stealing onions last evening.'

'Oh, was that his name?' the priest asked vaguely. 'Of course, I couldn't be sure he stole them. There were onions stolen all right, but that's a different thing.'

'But I understand you caught him in the act,' Howe said with a frown.

'Oh, no,' Father MacEnerney replied gravely. 'That's an exaggeration. I didn't actually catch him doing anything. I admit I charged him with it, but he denied it at once. At once!' he repeated earnestly, as though this might be an important point in the sentry's favour. 'It seemed, according to what he told me, that he saw some children in my garden and chased them away, and as they were running they dropped the onions I found. Those could be kids from the village, of course.'

'First I've heard of anybody from the village,' Howe said in surprise. 'Did you see any kids around, padre?'

'No,' Father MacEnerney admitted hesitatingly. 'I didn't see them, but that wouldn't mean they weren't there. They're always snooping around the camp. You know that.'

'I'll have to ask him about that,' said Howe. 'It is a point in his favour. I'm afraid it won't make much difference though. What really concerns us is that he deserted his post. He could be shot for that, of course.'

'Deserted his post?' Father MacEnerney repeated in consternation. This was worse than anything he had ever imagined. This was terrible! The wretched man might lose his life and for no reason except that a priest couldn't control his wicked temper. He felt he was being well punished for it. 'But how did he desert his post?'

'Well, you caught him in your garden,' Howe replied brus-

quely. 'In that time the whole camp could have been surprised and taken.'

In his distress the priest almost asked him not to talk
nonsense. As if a military camp in the middle of England
was going to be surprised and taken while the sentry nipped
into a nearby garden for a handful of onions! But that was
the English all out! They had to reduce everything to the
most literal terms.

'Oh, hold on now!' he said, raising a commanding hand.
'I think there must be a mistake. I never said I caught him
in the garden.'

'No, he said that,' Howe replied irritably. 'Didn't you?'

'Oh, no,' Father MacEnerney said emphatically, feeling
that casuistry was no longer any use. 'I certainly didn't. Are
you quite sure that man is right in his head?'

Fortunately for him, at this moment Elsie appeared with
the coffee and Father MacEnerney was able to watch her
and the coffee-pot instead of Howe, who, he knew, was
watching him closely enough. He only hoped he didn't look
the way he felt – like a particularly stupid criminal.

'Thanks,' Howe said, sitting back with his coffee-cup in
his hand. Then he went on remorselessly. 'Am I to understand that you beat this fellow up across the garden wall?'

'Listen, my friend,' Father MacEnerney said desperately.
'I tell you that man is never right in his head. He must be a
hopeless neurotic. They get like that, you know. Persecution
mania, they call it. He'd never talk that way if he had any
experience of being beaten up. I give you my word of honour
that it's the wildest exaggeration. I don't often raise my fist
to a man, but when I do, I leave evidence.'

'I can believe that,' Howe said with a cheeky grin.

'Now, I admit I did threaten to knock this fellow's head
off,' continued the priest, 'but that was when I thought he'd
taken my onions.' In his excitement he drew closer to Howe
till he was standing over him, a big bulky figure of a man,
and suddenly, to his astonishment, he felt the tears in his
eyes. 'Between ourselves, I behaved badly,' he said emotion-
ally. 'I don't mind admitting it to you, but I wouldn't like it
to get round. I have a terrible temper. An uncontrollable

temper. He threatened to give me in charge.'

'The little bastard!' Howe said with a surprise that contained a slight element of pleasure.

'And he'd have been perfectly justified,' the priest said earnestly. 'I had no right whatever to accuse him without a scrap of evidence. If I'd been in his shoes, I'd have taken the man who did it up to the guard room and made him repeat it. I behaved shockingly.'

'I shouldn't let it worry me too much,' Howe said cheerfully.

'I can't help it,' said the priest. 'I'm sorry to say the language I used was disgraceful. As a matter of fact, I had made up my mind to apologize next time I met him.'

He returned to his chair, almost weeping.

'This is one of the strangest cases I've ever dealt with,' Howe said. 'You don't think we're talking at cross purposes, do you? The chap you mean was tall and dark with a small moustache, isn't that right?'

For a moment Father MacEnerney felt a rush of relief at the thought that, after all, it was merely a case of mistaken identity. To mix it up a bit more was his immediate reaction. He did not see the trap until it was too late.

'That's right,' he said, and knew at once that it wasn't. Howe smiled and took his time. Then his long jaw shot up like a rat-trap.

'Why are you telling me all these lies, padre?' he asked quietly.

'Lies?' shouted Father MacEnerney, flushing.

'Lies, of course,' said Howe without pity or rancour. 'Damn lies! Transparent lies! You've been trying to fool me for the last ten minutes, and you very nearly succeeded. You're a very plausible liar, padre, but you can't take me in.'

'Ah, how can I remember?' Father MacEnerney said miserably. 'I don't know why you think I should attach so much importance to a handful of onions.'

'At present, I'm more interested in finding out what importance you attach to the rigmarole you've just told me,' said Howe. 'I presume you're trying to shield Collins. I'm blessed if I know why. I thought him a pretty nasty specimen, myself.'

Father MacEnerney did not reply. If Howe had been Irish, he would not have asked such a silly question, and, as he was not Irish, he wouldn't understand the answer. The MacEnerneys had all been like that. Father MacEnerney's father, the most truthful, God-fearing man he had known, had been threatened with a prosecution for perjury committed in the interest of a neighbour.

'Anyhow,' Howe went on sarcastically, 'what really happened was that you came home, found your garden had been robbed, said "Goodnight" to the sentry, and asked him who did it. He said it was some kids from the village, and then you probably had a long talk about the beautiful, beautiful moonlight. All very interesting. Now, what about coming up to the mess one night for dinner?'

'I'd love it,' the priest said boyishly. It was a great relief to know that Howe didn't really hold it against him. 'To tell you the God's truth, I'm destroyed here for someone to talk to.'

'Come on Thursday,' said Howe. 'And don't expect too much of the grub. It's a psychological conditioning for the horrors of modern war. But we'll give you lots of onions. I hope you don't recognize them.'

Then he went off, laughing. Father MacEnerney laughed too, but he didn't laugh long. It struck him that the English had a very peculiar sense of humour. To him, that interview had been anything but a joke. Here he was, a man who had always hated liars, and he had lied his own head off until even Howe despised him. That was queer conduct in a priest! He rang up the convent and asked for Sister Margaret. She was his principal confidant.

'Remember the sentry last night?' he asked in his gloomy, expressionless voice.

'Yes, father,' she said nervously. 'What about him?'

'He's after being arrested,' he said darkly.

'Oh!' she said. After a long pause she added: 'For what, father?'

'Stealing onions and being absent from duty. I had an officer here, making inquiries. It seems he could be shot.'

'Oh, father, isn't that awful?' she gasped.

' 'Tis bad,' he agreed.

'Oh, isn't that the English all out?' she cried. 'The rich can do what they like, and a poor man can be shot for stealing a few onions! I suppose it never crossed their minds that he might be hungry? Those poor fellows that never get a proper meal! What did you say?'

'Nothing.'

'You did right,' she said stormily. 'I'd have told them a pack of lies.'

'I did that too,' said Father MacEnerney.

'Oh, I don't believe for an instant that 'tis a sin, father,' she said hysterically. 'I don't care what anybody says about it. I'd say it in front of the Pope. I'm sure 'tis an act of charity.'

'That's what I thought too,' he said. 'It didn't go down too well though. But I liked the officer. I'll be seeing him again, and I think I might be able to get round him. The English are very good like that, when they get to know you.'

'I'll start a novena for the poor man at once,' she said firmly.

Travellers' Samples (1951)

DARCY IN THE LAND OF YOUTH

One

During the War when he was out of a job Mick Darcy went to England as clerk in a factory. He found the English as he had always supposed them to be: people with a great welcome for themselves and very little for anyone else.

Besides, there were the air-raids, which the English pretended not to notice. In the middle of the night Mick would be wakened by the wail of a siren and the thump of faraway guns, like all the windowpanes of heaven rattling. The thud of artillery, growing louder, accompanied a faint buzz like a cat's purring that seemed to rise out of a corner of the room and mount the wall to the ceiling, where it hung, breathing in steady spurts, exactly like a cat. Pretending not to notice things like that struck Mick as a bit ostentatious: he would rise and dress himself and sit lonesome by the gasfire, wondering what on earth had induced him to leave home.

The daytime wasn't much better. The works were a couple of miles outside the town, and he shared an office with a woman called Penrose and a Jew called Isaacs. Penrose addressed him as 'Mr Darcy' and when he asked her to call him 'Mick' she affected not to hear. Isaacs was the only one in the works who called him 'Mick', but it soon became plain that he only wanted Mick to join the Communist Party.

'You don't want to be a fellow traveller,' he said.

'No,' said Mick. 'I don't want to be a traveller at all.'

On his afternoons off, he took long, lonesome country walks, but there was nothing there you could describe as country either; only red-brick farms and cottages with crumpled oak frames and high, red-tiled roofs, big, sickly-looking fields divided by low neat hedges that made them look as though they all called one another by their surnames, and handsome-looking pubs named like The Star and Garter or The Shoulder of Mutton that were never open when you wanted them. No wonder he pined for Cork, his girl, Ina, and his great friend, Chris.

But it is amazing the effect even one girl can have on a feeling of home-sickness. Janet Fuller in Personnel was a tall, thin, fair-haired girl with a quick-witted laughing air. When Mick talked to her she listened with her head forward and her eyebrows raised expectantly. There was nothing in the least alarming about Janet, and she didn't seem to want to convert him to anything, so he asked her to have a drink with him. She even called him 'Mick' without being asked.

It was a great comfort. Now he had someone to talk to in his spare time, and he no longer felt scared of the country or the people. Besides, he had begun to master his job, and this always gave him a feeling of self-confidence. He even began to surprise the others at the factory. One day a group of them, including Janet, had broken off work for a chat when they heard the boss and scattered – even Janet said 'Goodbye' hastily. But Mick just gazed out of the window, his hands still in his trousers pockets, and when the boss came in, he saluted him over his shoulder. 'Settling in, Darcy?' the boss said in a friendly tone. 'Just getting the hang of things,' Mick replied modestly. Next day the boss sent for him, but it was only to ask his advice about something, and Mick gave it in his forthright way. If Mick had a weakness, it was that he liked to hear himself talk.

But he still continued to get shocks. One evening he had supper in the flat that Janet shared with a girl called Fanny, who was an analyst in one of the factories. Fanny was a good-looking dark haired girl with a tendency to moodiness. She asked how Mick was getting on with Mrs Penrose.

'Oh,' said Mick, 'she still calls me "Mr Darcy".'

'I suppose that's only because she expects to be calling you something else before long,' said Fanny gloomily.

'Oh, no, Fanny,' said Janet. 'You wouldn't know Penrose now. She's a changed woman. With her husband in Egypt, Peter posted to Yorkshire, and no one to play with but George, she's begun to talk about the simple pleasures of life. Penrose and primroses, you know.'

'Penrose?' Mick explained incredulously. 'I never thought she was that sort. Are you sure, Janet? I'd have thought she was an iceberg.'

'An iceberg!' Janet said gleefully, rubbing her hands. 'Oh, boy! A blooming fireship!'

Going home that night through the pitch-dark streets, Mick really felt at home for the first time. He had made friends with two of the nicest girls you could wish for – fine, broad-minded girls you could speak to as you'd speak to a man. He had to step into the roadway to make room for two other girls, flicking their torches on and off before them – schoolgirls, to judge by their voices. 'Of course, he's mar-

ried,' one of them said as they passed, and then went off into a rippling scale of laughter that sounded almost unearthly
in the silence and darkness.

A bit too broad-minded at times, perhaps, thought Mick,
coming to himself. For a while he did not feel quite so much
at home.

Two

In the spring evenings Janet and himself cycled off into
the nearby villages and towns for their drinks. Janet wanted
him to see the country. Sometimes Fanny came too, but she
did not seem so keen on it. It was as though she felt herself
in the way, yet when she did refuse to accompany them,
she looked after them with such a reproachful air that it
seemed to make Janet feel guilty.

One Sunday evening they went to church together. It
seemed to surprise Janet that Mick went to Mass every Sunday. She went with him once and clearly it did not impress
her. Her own religion seemed a bit mixed. Her father had
been a Baptist lay preacher and her mother a Methodist,
but Janet herself had fallen in love with a parson at the age
of eleven and remained Church till she joined the Socialist
Party at the age of eighteen. Most of the time she did not
seem to Mick to have any religion at all. She said that you
just died and rotted, and that was all anyone knew about
it, and this seemed to be the general view. There were any
amount of religions, but no beliefs you could put your finger
on.

Janet was so eager that he should go to church with her
that he agreed, though it was against his principles. It was
a little town ten miles from where they lived. Inside the
church was a young sailor playing the organ while another
turned over for him. The parson rang the bell himself, and
only three women turned up. The service itself was an awful
sell. The parson turned his back on them and read prayers
at the east window; the organist played a hymn, which the
three women and Janet joined in, and then the parson read

more prayers. However, it seemed to get Janet all worked up.

'Pity about Fanny,' she said when they were drinking beer in the inn yard later. 'We could be very comfortable in the flat only for her. Haven't you a friend who'd take her off our hands?'

'Only in Ireland.'

'Tell him I'll get him a job here. Say you've a nice girl for him as well. She really *is* nice, Mick.'

'Oh, I know,' said Mick. 'But hasn't she a fellow already?'

'Getting a fellow for Fanny is the great problem of my life,' Janet said ruefully.

'I wonder if she'd have him,' said Mick, thinking how nice it would be to have a friend as well as a girl. Janet was as good as gold, but there were times when Mick pined for masculine companionship.

'If he's anything like you, she'd jump at him,' said Janet.

'Oh, there's no resemblance,' said Mick who had never before been flattered like this and loved it. 'Chris is a holy terror.'

'A holy terror is what Fanny needs,' Janet said grimly.

It was only as time went by that he realized she was not exaggerating. Fanny was jealous; there was no doubt of that. She didn't intend to be rude, but she watched his plate as Janet filled it, and he saw that she grudged him even the food he ate. There wasn't much, God knows, and what there was, Janet gave him the best of, but all the same it was embarrassing. Janet did her best by making her feel welcome to join them, but Fanny only grew moodier.

'Oh, come on, Fanny!' Janet said one evening. 'I only want to show Mick the Plough in Alton.'

'Well, who'd know it better?' Fanny asked darkly, and Janet's temper blazed up.

'There's no need to be difficult,' she said.

'Well, it's not my fault if I'm inhibited, is it?' asked Fanny with a cowed air. Mick saw with surprise that she was terrified of Janet in a tantrum.

'I didn't say you were inhibited,' Janet replied in a stinging voice. 'I said you were difficult.'

'Same thing from your point of view, isn't it?' Fanny asked. 'Oh, I suppose I was born that way. You'd better let me alone.'

All the way out Janet was silent, and Mick saw she was still mad, though he couldn't guess why. He didn't know what Fanny meant when she said she was inhibited, or why she seemed to speak about it as if it were an infectious disease. He only knew that Janet had to be smoothed down.

'We'll have to get Chris for Fanny all right,' he said. 'An exceptional girl like that, you'd think she'd have fellows falling over her.'

'I don't think Fanny will ever get a man,' Janet said in a shrill, scolding voice. 'I've thrown dozens of them at her head, but she won't even make an effort to be polite. I believe she's one of those women who go through life without even knowing what it's about. She's just a raging mass of inhibitions.'

There it was again! Prohibitions, exhibitions, inhibitions! Mick wished to God Janet would use simple words. He knew what exhibitions were from one old man in the factory who had gone to gaol because of them, but if inhibitions meant the opposite, what was there to grouse about?

'Couldn't we do something about them?' he asked helpfully.

'Yes, darling,' she replied mockingly. 'Take her away to hell and give her a good roll in the hay. Then bring her back to me, human.'

Mick was so shocked he did not reply. By this time he was used to English dirty jokes, but he knew this wasn't just one of them. No doubt Janet was joking about the roll in the hay – though he wasn't too sure she was joking about that either – but she wasn't joking about Fanny. She really meant that all that was wrong with Fanny was that she was still a virgin, and that this was a complaint she did not suffer from herself.

The smugness of it horrified him as much as the savagery. Put in a certain way, it might be understandable and even forgivable. Girl of Janet's kind were known at home as 'damaged goods' but Mick had never permitted the expression to pass. He had a strong sense of justice and always took the side of the underdog. Some girls hadn't the same strength of character as others, he supposed; some were subjected to great temptations. He had never met any, to his knowledge, but he was quite sure that if he had he would have risen to the occasion. But a girl of that kind standing up and denouncing another girl's strength as weakness was too much for him altogether. It was like being asked to stand on his head.

Having got rid of her tantrum, Janet cheered up. 'This is wonderful,' she sighed with a tranquil pleasure as they floated downhill to Alton and the Plough – a pleasant little inn, standing by the bridge. Mick didn't feel it was so very wonderful. He had begun to wonder what Fanny had meant by asking who would know it better than Janet, and why Janet had lost her temper so badly. It sounded to him as though there had been some dirty work in connexion with it.

While Janet sat in the garden, he went to the bar for beer and stood there for a while unnoticed. There was a little group at the bar: a bald, fat man in an overcoat, smoking a pipe; a good-looking young man with a fancy waistcoat, and a local with a face like a turnip. The landlord, a man of about fifty, had a long, haggard face and wore horn-rimmed glasses; his wife, apparently twenty years younger, was a good-looking woman with bangs and a Lancashire accent. They never noticed Mick while they discussed a death in the village.

'I'm not against religion,' the man with the turnip face spluttered excitedly. 'I'm chapel myself, but I never tried to force my own views on people. All the months poor Harry was paralysed his wife and daughter never so much as wet his lips. That idn't right, is it? That idn't religion.'

'No, Bill,' said the landlord, shaking his head. 'Going too far, I call that.'

'That's fanaticism,' said the man with the pipe.

'Everyone is entitled to his own views, but them weren't old Harry's views, were they?' asked the man with the turnip face.

'No, Bill, they certainly weren't,' the landlord's wife said sadly.

'I'm for freedom, myself,' Bill said, tapping his chest. 'The night before he died, I come in here and got a quart of mild and bitter. Didn't I, Joe?'

'Mild, wadn't it, Bill?' the publican asked anxiously.

'No, Joe, mild and bitter was always Harry's drink.'

'Don't you remember, Joe?' the landlord's wife asked.

'Funny,' her husband replied sadly. 'I could have sworn it was mild.'

'Anyhow, I said to Millie and Sue, "All right," I said. "You run along to chapel, or wherever you want to go. I'll sit up with old Harry." Then I took out the bottle. His poor eyes lit up. Couldn't move, couldn't speak, but I shall never forget how he looked at that bottle. I had to hold his mouth open' – Bill threw back his head and pulled down one side of his mouth with his thumb – 'and let it trickle down. And was I pleased when he died next morning? I said to myself. "That man might have gone into his grave without a drink." No, if that's religion give me beer!'

'Wonder where old Harry is now,' the fat man said, removing his pipe reverently. 'Mystery, Joe, i'nt it?'

'Shocking!' the landlord said, shaking his head.

'We don't know, do we, Charles?' the landlady said sadly.

'Nobody knows,' Bill bawled scornfully as he took up his pint again. 'How could they? Parson pretends to know, but he don't know any more than you and me. Shove you in the ground and let the worms have you – that's all anybody knows.'

Mick was struck by the similarity of Janet's views with those of the people in the pub, and he felt you really couldn't expect much from any of them.

'Isn't it lovely here?' she said when he brought out the drinks.

'Very nice,' Mick said without much enthusiasm. You couldn't feel very enthusiastic about a place while you were wondering who else had been there with your girl.

'We must come and spend a few days here some time,' she said, and it made him more depressed than ever. 'You don't think I'm too bitchy about Fanny, do you, Mick?'

'It's not that,' he said. 'I wasn't thinking about Fanny in particular. Just about the way everybody in the factory seems to behave – fellows and girls going off together, as if they were going to a dance.'

'Having seen the factory, can you wonder?' she asked, and took a long drink of her beer.

'And when they get tired of one another they go off with someone else,' he said dryly. 'Or back to the number they started with. Like Hilda in the packing shed. She's tired of knocking round with Dorman, and when her husband comes back she's going to drop him. At least, she says she will.'

'Isn't that how these things usually end?' she asked.

'Oh, come on, Janet!' he said scornfully. 'You're not going to pretend there's nothing else to it.'

'I suppose like everything else, it's just what you choose to make it,' she said with a shrug.

'That isn't making much of it,' he said, beginning to grow heated. 'If it's only a roll in the hay, as you call it, there's nothing in it for anybody.'

'And what do you think it should be?' she asked with a frosty politeness that seemed to be the equivalent of his heat. He realized that he wasn't really keeping to the level of a general discussion. He could distinctly hear how common his accent had become, but excitement and a feeling of injury carried him away. He sat back stubbornly with his hands in his trousers pockets.

'But look here, Janet, learning to live with somebody isn't a thing you can pick up in a weekend. It's not a part-time job. You wouldn't take up a job somewhere in the middle, expecting to like it, and intending to drop it in a few months' time if you didn't.'

'Oh, Mick, don't tell me you have inhibitions too!' she said in mock distress.

'I don't know what they are and I don't care,' retorted Mick, growing commoner as he descended further from the heights of abstract discussion. 'And most of the people who use words like that have no idea of their meaning either.'

'Scruples, shall we say, so?' she asked, yielding the point.

'Well, we can agree on what they are,' he said.

'But after all, Mick, you've had affairs yourself, haven't you?' she added.

Now, this was a question Mick dreaded to answer, because, owing to a lack of suitable opportunities for which he was in no way to blame, he had not. For the matter of that, so far as he knew, none of his friends had either. But coming from a country where men's superiority – affairs or no affairs – was unchallenged, he did not like to admit that, so far as experience went, Fanny and he were in the one boat. He was even beginning to understand why poor Fanny felt such a freak.

'I'm not pretending I haven't,' he said casuistically.

'But then there's no argument, Mick,' she said with all the enthusiasm of a liberal mind discovering common ground with an opponent.

'No argument, maybe, but there are distinctions,' he said knowingly.

'Such as?'

'Oh, between playing the fool and being in love,' he replied as though he could barely bother to explain such matters to one as inexperienced as herself.

'The combination isn't altogether unknown either, is it?'

'The distinction seems to be, quite a bit,' he replied. 'To me, Penrose is one thing and you're another. Maybe I wouldn't mind having an affair with Penrose. God knows it's about all she's good for.'

'But you would with me?' she said, growing red.

'I would,' Mick said, realizing that the cat was out of the bag at last. 'I suppose it's a matter of responsibilities. If I make a friend, I don't begin by thinking what use I can make of him. If I fall in love with a girl I'm not going to begin calculating how cheap I can get her. I don't want anything cheap,' he added earnestly. 'I'm not going to rush into anything till I know the girl well enough to try and make a decent job of it. Is that plain?'

'Remarkably plain,' she said icily. 'You mean you're not that sort of man. Let me buy you a drink.'

'No, thanks.'

'Then I think we'd better be getting back,' she said, rising and looking like the wrath of God.

Mick, crushed and humiliated, followed her at a slouch, his hands still in his pockets. It wasn't good enough. At home a girl would have gone on with an argument like that till one of them fell unconscious, and in an argument Mick had real staying power, so he felt that she was taking an unfair advantage. Of course, he saw that she had some reason. However you looked at it, she had more or less told him she expected him to be her lover, and he had more or less told her that he was not that sort of man, and he had a suspicion that this was an entirely new experience for Janet. She might well feel mortified.

But the worst of it was that thinking it over, he realized that even then, he had not been quite honest. In fact, he had not been honest at all. He had not told her that he already had a girl at home. He believed all he had said, but he didn't believe it quite so strongly as all that – not so as to make exceptions. Given time, he might easily have made an exception of Janet. She was the sort of girl most men made an exception of. It was the shock that had made him express himself so bluntly; the shock of realizing that a girl he cared for had been the mistress of other men. He had reacted that way more in protest against them than against her.

But the real shock had been the discovery that he cared so much what she was.

Three

They never resumed the discussion openly, on those terms at least, and it seemed at times as though Janet had forgiven him, but only just. The argument was always there beneath the surface, ready to break out again if either lost his temper. It flared up for a moment whenever she mentioned Fanny – 'I suppose one day she'll meet an Irishman, and they'll spend the rest of their lives discussing their inhibitions.' And when she mentioned other men she had known, like Bill, with whom she had spent a holiday in Dorset, and an American called Tom, with whom she had gone to the Plough in Alton, she seemed to be contrasting a joyous past with a dreary present, and became cold and insolent.

Mick, of course, gave as good as he got. He had a dirty tongue when he chose to use it, and he had considerably more ammunition than she had. The canteen was always full of gossip about who was living with whom, and whose wife (or husband) had returned and found him (or her) in bed with somebody else, and he passed it on with an air of amused contempt. The first time she said 'Good!' in a ringing voice: afterwards, she contented herself with a shrug. Mick suggested helpfully that perhaps it took all those religions to deal with as many scandals, and she retorted that, no doubt, one religion would be more than enough for Ireland.

All the same, he could not help feeling that it wasn't nice. He remembered what Fanny had said about the Plough. Really, really, it wasn't nice! It seemed to show a complete lack of sensibility in Janet to bring him to a place where she had stayed with another man, and it made him suspicious of every other place she brought him.

Still, he could not do without her, nor, apparently, could she do without him. They met every evening after work, went off together on Saturday afternoons, and even went to Mass together on Sunday mornings.

As a result, before he went home on leave, everything seemed to have changed between them. She no longer made snooty remarks about Fanny's virginity and ceased to refer to Bill and Tom altogether. Indeed, from her conversation it would have been hard to detect that she had ever known such men, much less been intimate with them. Mick wondered whether it wasn't possible for a woman to be promiscuous and yet remain innocent, and decided regretfully that it wasn't. But no wife or sweetheart could have shown more devotion in the last week before his holiday, and when they went to the station together and walked arm-in-arm to the end of the long draughty platform, she was stiff with unspoken misery. She seemed to feel it was her duty to show no sign of emotion, either.

'You will come back, Mick, won't you?' she asked.

'Why?' Mick replied banteringly. 'Do you think you can keep off Americans for a fortnight?'

Janet spat out a horrible word that showed only too clearly her familiarity with Americans and others. It startled and shocked Mick. It seemed that the English had strong ideas about when you could joke and when you couldn't, and this was apparently not a time for joking. To his surprise, he found her trembling all over.

At any other time he would have argued with her, but already he was, in spirit and least, halfway home. Beyond the end of the line was Cork, and meat and butter and nights of unbroken sleep. When he leaned out of the window to wave goodbye she was standing like a statue, looking curiously desolate.

He didn't reach home until the following evening. Since he had told no one of his arrival he came in an atmosphere of sensation. He shaved, and, without waiting for more than a cup of tea, set off down the road to Ina's. Ina was the youngest of a large family, and his arrival there created a sensation too. Elsie, the eldest, a fat jolly girl just home from work, shouted with laughter at him.

'He smelt the sausages!' she said.

'You can keep your old sausages,' Mick said scornfully. 'I'm taking Ina out to dinner.'

'You're what?' asked Elsie. 'You have high notions like the goats in Kerry.'

'But I have to make my little brothers' supper, honey,' Ina said laughingly, smoothing his hair. She was a slight, dark, radiant girl with a fund of energy.

'Tell them to make it themselves,' said Mick.

'Tell them, you!' cried Elsie. 'Someone should have told them years ago, the caubogues! They're thirty, and they have no more intention of marrying than of flying. Have you e'er an old job for us over there? I'm damned for want of a man.'

Ina, surprised at Mick's firmness, rushed upstairs to change. Her two brothers came in, expressed astonishment at Mick's arrival, satisfaction at his promotion, incredulity at his opinion that the English were not beaten already, and consternation that their supper was not on the table. They began hammering together with their knives and forks.

'Supper up!' shouted the elder. 'We can't wait all night. Where the hell is Ina?'

'Coming out to dinner with me,' Mick said with a sniff, feeling that for once he was uttering a curtain line.

They called for Chris – an undersized lad with a pale face like a fist and a voice like melted butter. He expressed great pleasure at seeing them, but gave no sign of it, because it was part of Chris's line not to be impressed by anything. He had always regarded Mick as a bit of a softy because of Ina. For himself, he would never keep a girl for more than a month because it gave her ideas.

'Ah, what do you want going to town for supper for?' he drawled incredulously, as if this were only another indication that Mick was not quite right in the head. 'Can't ye have it at home? 'Twon't cost ye anything.'

'You didn't change much anyway,' Mick said dryly. 'Hurry up, or we won't get anything at all.'

Next morning, in bed, Mick got a letter from Janet that must have been written while he was still on the train. She said that trying to face things without him was like trying to get used to an amputated limb: she kept on making movements before realizing that it wasn't there. At that point, Mick dropped the letter with a sigh. He wished English people wouldn't write like that. It sounded so unreal.

He wished he could remain at home, but didn't see how he could do it, without a job. Instead, he started to coax Chris into coming back with him. He knew that his position in the factory would guarantee a job for anyone who did. Besides, he had grown tired of Ina's brothers telling him how the Germans would win the war. He had never been very interested in the war or who won it, and was surprised to hear himself replying in Chris's cynical drawl,

'They will, and what else?' Ina's brothers were equally surprised. They had not expected Mick to turn his coat so
quickly.

'People here never seem to talk of anything only religion
and politics,' he said one night to Chris as they were walking up the Western Road.

'And what better could they talk about?' asked Chris.
'Damn glad you were to get back to them! You can get a
night's rest anyway.'

'There's no one to stop you,' Mick said.

Chris stared at him, uncertain whether or not Mick meant
what he seemed to mean. Like most other friends, they had
developed throughout the years along a pattern of standard
reaction in which Mick had played the innocent, Chris the
worldly one. Now, Mick seemed to be developing out of
his knowledge entirely.

'Go on!' he said with a cautious grin. 'Are they as good-
natured as that?'

'I didn't want to say it,' said Mick modestly. 'But I've the
very girl for you.'

'You don't say so!' Chris exclaimed, with a smile of a
child who has ceased to believe in Santa Claus but likes to
hear about it just the same.

'Grand-looking girl with a good job and a flat of her own,'
said Mick. 'What more do you want?'

Chris suddenly beamed.

'I wouldn't let Ina hear me talking like that if I was you,'
he said. 'Some of them quiet-looking girls are a terrible
hand with a hatchet.'

At that moment it struck Mick with cruel force how little
Ina or anybody else had to reproach him with. They were
passing by the college, and groups of clerks and servant
girls were strolling by, whistling and calling. He was sure
there wasn't another man in Ireland who would have behaved as stupidly as he had done. He remembered Janet
at the railway station with her desolate air, and her letter,
which he had not answered, and which, perhaps, she had
really meant. A bloody fool!

Suddenly everything seemed to turn upside down on him.

He was back in the bar in Alton, listening to the little group discussing the dead customer while he waited to carry the drinks out to Janet on the rustic seat in the garden, feeling that she was unreal and faithless. Now, it wasn't she who seemed unreal, but the Western Road and the clerks and servant girls who just didn't know what they wanted. They were a dream from which he had wakened; a dream from which he had wakened before without even realizing that he was awake.

He was so shaken that he almost told Chris about Janet, but he knew that Chris wouldn't understand him any more than he had understood himself. Chris would talk sagaciously of 'damaged goods', as if there were only one way a woman could be damaged.

'I have to go back to town, Chris,' he said, stopping. 'I just remembered a telephone call I have to make.'

'Fair enough,' Chris said, with an understanding that surprised him. 'I suppose you might as well tell her I'm coming too.'

Four

Outside, against the clear summer sky, shadowy figures moved with pools of light at their feet and searchlights flickered like lightning over the battlements of the castle. Chris groaned and Mick gripped his arm confidently.

'This is nothing,' he said. 'Probably only a scouting plane. You get lots of them around here. Wait till they start dropping a few wagons of high explosive!'

It was a real pleasure to Mick to hear himself talk in that way. He seemed to have become forceful and cool all at once. It had something to do with Chris's being there, as though this had given his protective instincts full scope. But there was something else as well; something he could not have believed possible. It was almost as though he were arriving home. Home, he felt, was a funny thing for him to think of at a time like that.

There was no raid, so he brought Chris round to the girls'

flat, and Chris groaned again at the channel of star-shaped traffic signals that twinkled between the black cliffs of houses, whose bases opened so mysteriously to reveal pale stencilled signs or caverns of smoky light.

Janet opened the door, gave one hasty, incredulous glance at Chris, and then hurled herself at Mick. Chris opened his eyes with a start – he later admitted to Mick that he had never before seen a doll so quick off the mark – but Mick no longer minded what he saw. While Chris and Fanny were in the throes of starting a conversation, he followed Janet into the kitchen, where she was recklessly tossing a week's rations into the frying pan. She was hot and excited, and she used two dirty words in succession, but they did not disturb him either. He leaned against the kitchen wall with his hands in his trousers pockets and smiled at her.

'Glad to see me?' he said.

'You should try this god-damn grease!' she said, rubbing her hand.

'I'm afraid you'll find I've left my principles behind me this time,' he said.

'Oh, good!' she said, not as enthusiastically as you might expect, but Mick put that down to the burn.

'What do you think of Chris?'

'A bit quiet, isn't he?' she asked doubtfully.

'Scared,' said Mick with a sniff. 'So would you be if your first glimpse of a country was in the middle of an alert. He'll get over that. Should we go off somewhere for the week-end?'

'Next weekend?'

'Or the one after. I don't mind.'

'You are in a hurry, aren't you?'

'So would you be, too, if you'd spent a fortnight in Cork.'

'And Fanny as well?'

'Why not? The more the merrier. Let's go somewhere really good. Take the bikes and make a proper tour of it. I'd like Chris to see a bit of the real country.'

It certainly did make a difference, having someone else there to think for. And a fortnight later, the four of them set off on bicycles out of town. Landscape and houses gradu-

ally changed about them, and old brick and flint gave place
to houses of small yellow stones, tinted with golden moss.
Out of the woven pullovers of wall rose gables with coifs of
tile. It all came over Mick in a rush; the company of a friend
and of his girl and a country he felt he had mastered.
This was what it really meant to feel at home. When
the others sat on a bench outside a country public-house,
Mick brought out the beer and smiled with the pride of
ownership.

'Good?' he asked Chris.

'The beer isn't much, if that's what you mean,' said Chris,
who still specialized in not being impressed.

In the late evening they reached their destination, and
dismounted in the cobbled yard of an inn where, according
to Janet, Queen Elizabeth was supposed to have stayed. At
either end of the dining room there was an oak dresser full
of willow-ware, with silvery sauceboats on the shelves and
brass pitchers on top.

'You'd want to mind your head in this hole,' Chris said
resentfully.

'But this place is four hundred years old, man,' said Mick.

'You think in that time they'd make enough to rebuild
it,' said Chris.

He was still acting in character, but Mick was just a little
disappointed in him. Fanny had been thrown into such a
panic that she was prepared to hit it off with anybody, but
Chris seemed to have lost a lot of his dash. Mick was not
quite sure yet that he would not take fright before Fanny,
but he would certainly do so if he knew what a blessed innocent she was. Whenever Mick looked at her, her dark sullen
face broke into a wistful smile that made him think of a
Christian martyr's first glimpse of the lion.

After supper Janet showed them round the town and
finally led them to a pub that was on no street at all but was
approached by a complicated system of alleyways. The
little bar room was full, and Janet and he were crowded into
the yard, and sat there on a bench in the starlight. Behind
the clutter of old tiled roofs a square battlements tower rose
against the sky.

'You're certain Fanny will be all right with Chris?' Janet asked anxiously.

'Oh, certain!' said Mick, wondering if his troops had opened negotiations with the enemy behind his back. 'Why? Did she say anything?'

'No, but she's in a flat spin,' Janet said, clucking with mother solicitude. 'I've told her everything I could think of, but she's still afraid she's got it wrong. If anyone could, that damn girl will. He does understand how innocent she is, doesn't he?'

'Oh, perfectly,' said Mick, feeling that his troops were already sufficiently out of hand. If Janet started giving them orders, they would undoubtedly cut and run.

Back in the bedroom, Chris was so depressed that it came almost as a relief to Mick, because he had no time to worry about himself. Then the handle of the door turned softly, and Janet tiptoed in in her bathing-wrap, her usual, competent, cool self as though arriving in men's bedrooms at that hour of night were second nature to her. 'Ready, Chris?' she whispered. Chris was a lad of great principle and Mick could not help admiring his spirit. With a face like death on him he went out, and Janet cautiously closed the door behind him. Mick listened to make sure he didn't hide in the lavatory. Then Janet switched off the light, drew back the black-out curtain, and shivering slightly, opened the window on the dark inn yard.

Five

When Mick woke up and realized where he was he felt an extraordinary peace. It was as though he had laid down some heavy burden he had been carrying all his life. The pleasantest part of it was that the burden was quite unnecessary, and that he had lost nothing by laying it down.

With a clarity that seemed to be another part of his happy state, he realized that all the charm of the old town had only been a put-up job of Janet's. Clearly, she had been

here already with another man. He should have known it
when she took them to the pub. That, too, was her reason
for choosing this pleasant old inn. She had stayed there
with someone else. It was probably the American, and it
might well be the same bed. Women had no interest in
scenery or architecture unless they had been made love to
in them, and this showed a certain amount of good sense.
They brought one man there because they had been happy
with another there. Happiness – that was the secret the
English had and the Irish lacked.

He didn't feel quite so sure of this when he realized that
what had waked him was Janet's weeping. There she was,
crying quietly beside him in the bed. It alarmed him, because he knew that in his innocence he might easily have
done something wrong.

'What is it, Jan?' he asked at last.

'Oh, nothing,' she said, dabbing her nose viciously with
her handkerchief. 'Go to sleep!'

'But how can I with you like that?' he asked plaintively.
'Was it something I did?'

'No, of course not, Mick. I'm just a fool, that's all.'

The wretchedness in her voice made him forget his
doubts of himself and think of her worries. Being a man of
the world was all right, but Mick would always be more at
home with other people's troubles. He put his arm round her
and she sighed and threw a bare leg over him. It embarrassed him, but he reminded himself that he was now a
man of the world.

'Tell me,' he said as though he were talking to a child.

'Oh, it's only what you said that night at the Plough,' she
sobbed.

'The Plough?'

'The Plough at Alton.'

Mick found it impossible to remember what he had said
at the Plough, except that it was probably something silly;
but he was used to the way women had of remembering
things some man had said and forgotten, and which he
would be glad if they had forgotten too.

'Remind me,' he said.

'Oh, when you said that love was a matter of responsibility.'

'Oh, yes, I remember,' he said, but he didn't. What he remembered mostly was that she had more or less told him about the other men and he had been hurt and angry. Now that he was no longer hurt and angry he didn't want to be reminded of what he had said. 'But you shouldn't take it so seriously, Jan.'

'What else could I do but take it seriously?' she asked fiercely. 'Of course I was mad with you for telling me the truth about myself, but I knew you were right. That was the way I'd always felt myself, only I blinded myself, just as you said; taking up love like a casual job I could drop when I pleased. Now I'm well paid for my bloody stupidity.'

She began to sob again, bitterly. Mick felt completely lost. If only the damn situation would stay steady long enough for him to get used to it! He had felt he understood this strange country, and now he realized he hadn't understood it at all. He had accepted all it had to teach him, and now all he got for his pains was to be told that he had been right all the time, and had only made a fool of himself in changing.

'Oh, of course, that's all perfectly true, Janet, but you can take it to the fair,' he said weakly. 'You should see some of the things I've seen at home in the last couple of weeks.' He hadn't really seen anything, and he knew he was making it up, but the warmth of his feelings made it seem as though he had seen nightmares. 'People brought up to look at the physical facts of love as something inhuman and disgusting! If they must believe in some sort of nonsense, it would be better for them to believe in the fairies, as they used to do.'

'Yes, but if I had a daughter, I'd prefer to bring her up like that than in the way I was brought up, Mick. At least, she'd be capable of being serious about something. What can I be serious about? I made fun of Fanny because she didn't sleep round like the rest of us, but if Fanny falls for Chris, the joke will be on me.'

'You don't mean you didn't want to come, all the time?' he asked in consternation.

'It's not that,' she said, beating her forehead with her fist. 'But can't you see that I wanted to prove to myself that I could be a decent girl for you, and that I wasn't one of the factory janes you made fun of? All right. You're not like the others, but how am I to show you? How do you know I won't be back here with another fellow in a couple of weeks time? I wanted to give you something worth while, and now I have nothing to give you.'

'I wouldn't say that, you know,' Mick said in embarrassment, but he really didn't know what else to say. Clearly this was another of these extraordinary occasions when the aeroplane you had been travelling so comfortably in turned upside down, and you were hanging on to your seat for fear of going through the roof. Here he had been for a glorious hour or so, feeling himself the hell of a fellow, and now he was back where he started, a plain, dull, decent lad again. He did not want to say it, but he knew he was going to say it anyway, and he did.

'We can always get married, you know.'

This threw Janet into something like convulsions, because if she did marry him she would never have the opportunity of showing him what she was really like, and it took him a long time to persuade her that he had never thought of her as anything but a serious-minded girl – most of the time, anyhow. Then she gave a deep sigh and fell asleep in the most awkward manner on his chest. Outside, the dawn was painting the old roofs and walls in the stiff artless colours of a child's paint-box. He felt a little bit lonely, a little bit sorry for himself. He knew that Chris would be furious and with good reason. As a man of the world he was a complete wash-out. He would have liked to remain a man of the world at least for a few months until it came natural to him, and he could scoff at conventions and pretensions from some sort of background of experience.

But it wasn't in his character, and you couldn't escape your character wherever you were or whatever you did. Marriage, it seemed, came more natural to him.

FRANK O'CONNOR

'A master' – *The Listener*

'Perfect' – *Spectator*

'No Irish writer perceives the Irish so subtly' – *The Guardian*

Two volumes of short stories by this master craftsman are now available from Pan Books. Both were originally published in one volume by Macmillan as Collection Two.

You must also read the enthralling and entrancing story of O'Connor's life from schoolboy to revolutionary to librarian and his association with the Abbey Theatre.

WALTER MACKEN

was born in Galway in 1915 and became one of Ireland's best loved writers. At his death in 1968 he left a number of unpublished short stories which are now reprinted with the best stories.

Also available in Pan is the fictional trilogy about Ireland's troubled history which was Walter Macken's finest achievement.

SEAN O'CASEY

'One of the most uncomfortable and memorable works of the century'
Eric Gillett

Sean O'Casey wrote his first evocative and richly entertaining autobiography in six volumes over more than two decades, recreating in Volume I the days of his Dublin childhood. The second volume tells of his coming to manhood and includes episodes later used in his play RED ROSES FOR ME. Each volume is essential reading for a proper appreciation of this major Irish dramatist.

I KNOCK ON THE DOOR
Autobiography Volume I   30p

PICTURES IN THE HALLWAY
Autobiography Volume II   30p

'A magnificent undertaking splendidly finished.'–*The Times*

A zestful welcome to the world of the Emerald Isle

A TASTE OE IRELAND

Theodora Fitzgibbon

A magnificent and truly delectable range of Irish traditional recipes are here collected together and illustrated with a most remarkable series of historic photographs, many of them over one hundred years old.

'A feast of a book' – *Ulster Tatler*

'The most charming cookery book of the year' – *Daily Mail*

A SELECTION OF POPULAR READING

Fiction

TRAMP IN ARMOUR	Colin Forbes	30p
SIEGE	Edwin Corley	35p
THE ROTTEN APPLE	Christopher Dilke	25p
EMBASSY	Stephen Coulter	30p
AIRPORT	Arthur Hailey	37½p
REQUIEM FOR A WREN	Nevil Shute	30p
THE AGGRAVATIONS OF MINNIE ASHE	Cyril Kersh	25p
THE ROSE AND THE SWORD	Sandra Paretti	40p
HEIR TO FALCONHURST	Lance Horner	40p
CATHERINE AND A TIME FOR LOVE	Juliette Benzoni	35p
A CASE OF NEED	Jeffery Hudson	35p

Non-Fiction

THE SOMERSET & DORSET RAILWAY (illus.)	Robin Atthill	35p
THE WEST HIGHLAND RAILWAY (illus.)	John Thomas	35p
LIFE AT THE LIMIT (illus.)	Graham Hill	35p
MY BEAVER COLONY (illus.)	Lars Wilsson	25p
THE PETER PRINCIPLE	Dr. Laurence J. Peter & Raymond Hull	30p
SILENCE ON MONTE SOLE	Jack Olsen	35p
THE NINE BAD SHOTS OF GOLF (illus.)	Jim Dante & Leo Diegel	35p
MISS READ'S COUNTRY COOKING	Miss Read	30p

These and other advertised PAN Books are obtainable from all booksellers and newsagents. If you have any difficulty please send purchase price plus 5p postage to P.O. Box 11, Falmouth, Cornwall. While every effort is made to keep prices low, it is sometimes necessary to increase prices at short notice. PAN Books reserve the right to show new retail prices on covers which may differ from those previously advertised in the text or elsewhere.